Black Cats & Pointy Hats

A LIMITED EDITION CHARITY ANTHOLOGY

JENÉE ROBINSON   **JUPITER DRESDEN**   **M. CALDER**

MK SAVAGE   **REBEL MORELLI**

ILLUSTRATED BY
EVE GRAPHIC DESIGN LLC.

Mission 22
Thank you for all you do for our Veterans and their families.

Contents

UNLUCKY

CATNIP & HIJINX

LOVE SPELLS AND WHISKER WHISPERS

ARCADIA

Unlucky

BY: JENÉE ROBINSON

CHAPTER *One*

THE ENCOUNTER-DID I SPILL THAT ON YOUR SHOES?

"Lucky!" my mother shrieks my name from the other side of the store.

Fuck, what did I do this time? I leave my spot at the front counter and disappear into the stacks of books that line the store. My mother and sisters ensured that he was pristine. All the shelves were glass, so I usually stuck to the register. Taking care with each step, because if I knock over another display it will be my hide that'll have bruises.

"Lucky!" Her voice resonates in my ears.

"Yes, Mother?" I ask in a light tone.

"Did you arrange these like this?" she asks, referring to the color-coded crystals on the glass shelves. Some artist has moved the beige ones into the shape of a penis.

I have to conceal my laugh as I say, "It wasn't me. I'm forbidden from even stepping into this section."

She is about to speak when the front door chimes. "Get back to the register, fast."

"Yes, Mother," I reply with a little nod.

With care, I move as fast as I dare. Twice, I have stopped myself from knocking over the books and I breathe a little easier when I'm back standing in my spot behind the counter.

"Welcome to Unlucky Seven," I greet the two women that had entered when I was chatting with my mother.

"What brings you in today?" I ask in a cheerful tone.

My smile fades when I notice that one of them has a tear-stained face.

"I thought some of your teas or crystals might help my sister get over her break up. What do you suggest for a broken heart?"

"Revenge," my sister, Mila, speaks up as she steps up beside me.

Both the patrons' eyes go wide at her words. "Excuse me?" the crying one asks.

"I'm only joking, but I'll be happy to help you find something that may help. I know it's an old saying, but the truth is, time is the healer of wounds," Mila notes.

She isn't wrong, but I don't move as Mila wraps an arm around the woman's shoulder and guides her deeper into the store.

I pull my book from under the counter and resume where I left off yesterday. Reading is the one thing I can do without fearing I will screw up or knock something over. At first, my mother told me she wouldn't allow it, but once she realized that it was best for me to stay in one place, she let me continue.

"What are you reading today?" Coral, my oldest sister asks. Her flaming-red hair is framing her face with curls.

I swear my sisters were blessed by the goddess with all the good traits and I was cursed. But that's what happens when you are the seventh daughter born to a family of witches. My family always believed that seven was a lucky number but once I was born, all that changed.

Before showing Coral the cover, I replace my bookmark. I just got to the climax of the book and don't want to forget where I am and wouldn't you know when I hand the book over, the slip of paper floats to the floor.

"Shit, I'm sorry, Lucky," Coral says, lowering her gaze.

"It's just par for the course. Don't even worry about it. I have a general idea where I was in the book," I state as she passes it back.

The door chimes again, but I don't have to look up to know that it's Coral's boyfriend. The way she slides from behind the counter and does a little squeak says it all.

"Wes, it's about time," she says as he wraps his arms around her waist.

I think I just threw up in my mouth a little. Why they can't wait until they are outside to get all handsy is beyond me. They don't mean to rub it in, at least I don't think they do, because with this curse, I'll never know love like that.

"Tell Mom I'll be back in time to close up," Coral says from over her shoulder as she and Wes make their way to the front door.

I give her a little nod and open my book, rifling through to find the page I was on. Just as I dive back into the world of vampires and dragons, the door chimes again for the third time since opening. That has to be some kind of record, even in October.

I repeat my greeting but don't gaze up from my book, that is until a deep-baritone voice says, "Hello."

I'm so startled that I knock over the potion that my mother said was a good advertisement. But she forgot one thing, I manned the counter and now this gorgeous man has 'love potion' all over his shoes.

"Oh my goddess, I'm so sorry," my words are rushed as I grab the dusting rag and move around the counter with ease.

"Did I spill that on your shoes?" I ask as I duck down to wipe it off him and the floor.

"Miss, it's okay, really. I didn't mean to scare you. I was just looking for some sage and a few crystals for my new place. Can you help me find that?" he asks as I stand with a handful of glass.

"Give me a moment and I'll have my sister, Crystal, help. As you can see I'm a walking disaster," I comment as I deposit the shards into the little bin I keep near the counter. I pull my phone from my pocket and start to text Crystal when he lays a hand on top of mine.

I glance up into his piercing, blue eyes as he says, "I think you will do just fine."

"Don't be too sure about that," I retort with a smile. "But if you like to live dangerously, follow me."

We navigate the books without me bumping into anything, but the ingredients are the next section that we're headed to, there's always a chance that I'll still fuck up. It isn't as hazardous as the crystals but it's a close second.

Some of the ingredients are in baskets on glass shelves and others hang from the ceiling as we let them dry.

"What kind of sage are you shopping for? Do you want a smudge stick? If so, we have seven different kinds."

"Seven?" he questions. "Usually when I go into a shop they just grab one and send me on my way."

"Then you haven't been going to the right shop," I snark before I can stop myself.

I glance at him and notice that blush on his cheeks.

"I...um...," I tried to backpedal. "I didn't mean it that way. It upsets me that people just try to make a quick buck and they aren't really helping anyone."

"I get that, just not most people are so frank and would take my money without a second thought. It's nice to see that you aren't like most people."

"You can say that again," I comment under my breath, looking back at the ground. "So, can you tell me what you want the sage to do? Clean negative energy? Hate? Healing? Purification? Rituals? Insects? Exorcisms?"

"Sage can really help with Exorcisms?" He laughs.

Well, that is until I gaze at him and he can see that I'm serious.

It's his turn to back peddle. "Oh…um…cleansing negative energy. I guess."

"So, white sage is what I'd suggest. That's its main purpose as a smudging stick," I say as I go to reach for a stick at the same time he does. There is a spark as our fingers touch for a mere second and we both jump back a little. But just my luck, I hit a shelf behind me, starting a domino effect as ingredients and wood go flying.

"Shit, Mom is gonna have my head," I mutter, watching in horror as the mess unfolds. Most people would jump into action but I have learned, after all these years, it's best to let it happen and then clean up the aftermath.

"I can help you clean this up," the stranger offers.

"No, it's my mess. Let's get your sage and I'll get my sister to help with the crystals." I smile up at him.

I grab a couple of sticks of the white sage and lead him back to the counter when Crystal and Tori meet us there.

"What happened?" they ask in unison.

"I did," I say flatly, "Crystal, can you please show him the crystals? I have a mess to clean before Mom returns from the bank."

She nods and tells him to follow her and they disappear into the corner.

"What really happened?" Tori questions, her stern gaze burning into me.

"I did, he asked for some sage and we figured out what kind he needed. We reached for the sticks at the same time and when our fingers grazed, I felt a shock and jumped back into the shelves behind us."

"A shock? Hmm…that's interesting," she comments.

"Will you help me with the damage? Mother's already in a mood because someone is making penis art again. She'll torture me if she sees the mess I've made," I plead with her.

"Of course. You didn't ask for this curse, Lucky, and I know that you are careful when you do go into the shop. So, there has to be something more with this mystery man, and he is gorgeous," Tori smirks.

She isn't wrong. He's about six foot, with sandy-blond hair, a sharp jawline, and those eyes, but I couldn't think more about him now.

"That he is," I say as Tori takes my hand and we head back to where the wreckage awaits.

"You sure did a number back here. If it wasn't for those cameras, we could magic it up in no time. Why these humans think security systems are a good idea is something I don't agree with. I know that if we were robbed that would serve a purpose but they are more of a nuisance, I think," Tori complains as she starts to collect items and arrange them.

Again, she had a point, I wasn't sure if that was the real reason that Mom had them installed but it did stop my sisters and I from openly using magic in the store.

I start righting the shelves when the front door chimes, I look at Tori and she motions for me to go, so I do.

Once I'm back at the counter, I notice that it is the local mean girls that have entered, milling around the tarot card and books that we keep up front.

"See, I told you she was a freak," the closest one hisses.

"Welcome to Unlucky Seven. Can I help you today?" I ask with a fake smile plastered on my face.

"From you, no," another one comments.

"Well, if you need some assistance please just let me or one of my sisters know," I say, trying to pretend that her words didn't sting. This is why I hate customer service, these bitches know that I'll be nice no matter how awful they are to me. I mean there are lines that they don't cross, so my hands are tied and I have to endure them.

The last one is about to make a comment—hateful, I'm sure—but her words stop as my sister returns with a handful of crystals and the handsome man.

"Is that all?" I ask as I punch the items into the computer.

He smiles at me, "For today, yes. You and your sister have been very helpful. I will definitely be back once I'm more settled.

"That's wonderful to hear," I say before giving him his total and bagging his items. "Thank you for shopping at Unlucky Seven. Come back soon."

He nods in return, taking his things, and all of us watch him leave.

"Eww, do you really think that hottie will go for you, Freak?" the blonde girl asks.

"I think it's time for you to leave," Crystal grits out. "We don't take kindly to cruelty here. This is a place of peace and healing."

"As if we would buy your dollar-store junk," another one states with a hair flip, dropping whatever she was holding to the floor.

The three of them don't make a scene as they leave, but I hold my breath until they disappear out the front door.

"Bitches," Crystal huffs.

I nod in agreement. "Can you watch the counter? I can't let Tori clean up my mess alone."

Crystal clasps me on the shoulder, "Lucky, we both know it's better for me to help Tori and you to stand here. For all of us and the store, really."

She gives a little laugh at the look on my face. "Really, you mean well but let me go. Besides, if Mom returns it's less suspicious if you are at the counter."

"I know you're right, I just hate being so unlucky."

CHAPTER
Two

HE RETURNS-ARE YOU SURE YOU MEANT ME?

It has been a couple of days since the hot stranger came in, but also the mean girls haven't shown their faces again. That is until today.

"Welcome to Unlucky Seven," I call from the counter, still reading my book. Once I get to the bottom of the page, I glance up and notice it is just the one quiet girl from the other day.

"Hi, I just wanted to come back in and apologize for my friends the other day. They really are good people, just not always the nicest," she states.

"Seems you are in need of some new friends," I comment as I replace my bookmark and close my book.

"It's hard to do when our mothers are best friends and they do everything together. I have to play nice even if I don't want to," she confesses.

"You're stuck between a rock and a hard place, huh?" I question with my eyebrow raised at her.

"Yeah, but that doesn't excuse their behavior. I am truly sorry," she says, biting her lip.

"It's all forgiven. I do suggest a crystal or two for all the negative energy you have with them," I offer.

"They would never let me live it down if I carried crystals with me." She sighs.

I let out a little laugh, "What if they were disguised in jewelry?'"

Her face lights up at that idea, "That's genius. What do you recommend?"

"Let me text one of my sisters and we will be happy to help you get all sorted out," I say as I reach for my phone.

"You can't show me them?" This time, I noticed a little sadness in her tone.

"Well, my name may be Lucky, but I'm just the opposite. I don't dare walk around the shop much and where we keep the crystals is off limits," I explain as I text my sister.

"So, are you the Unlucky in the Unlucky Seven?" she asks.

I give her a little nod as my sister, Jupiter, has arrived as my backup.

"Jupiter, can you help her find some jewelry that has crystals infused with warding off negative energy?"

My sister gives me a little smile, "Of course. We can't have you wreaking havoc on that section of the store, can we?"

I knew that she wasn't trying to be mean, but it didn't stop the sting of her words.

"Nope, after the sage and stuff the other day, I'm still trying to get back on Mom's good side," I reply and open my book back up as Jupiter takes the customer off toward the crystals.

I've read two pages and am almost at the bottom of the third when the door chimes again. I mark my place and spout the normal greeting.

"Do they ever let you out from behind that counter?"

Damn it, his voice shakes me again. But luckily for me, I had already moved all the breakables out of my reach. I didn't want to spill anything on another customer if I was startled again.

"What?" I ask.

"Are you always behind the counter?" he repeats.

"That I am, because I can contain my destruction zone to a minimum," I say honestly.

"Are you really that unlucky?" he asks.

"My mother even named me Lucky, to try and counteract some of the negative energy," I answer, before slapping my hand over my mouth. I've said too much, why am I telling him all of this? I don't even know his name.

"Well, Lucky, I'm Felix. It's nice to meet you," Felix says, holding out a hand toward me.

I start to take it but pull back at the last second. I know it's silly but what if my misfortune rubs off on this man?

"What? I promise my hands are clean," he says with his hand still out.

"Well, if my lack of luck rubs off on you, that's all on you," I inform him as I take his hand to shake it.

The moment our palms touch, there is a little spark and we both jump back. I bump into the shelves behind me, knocking ancient books to the floor, so I start gathering them up. I'm just grateful that none of the books show any signs of damage.

"Can I help you with that?" Felix questions.

"No, no. What can I help you with? I figure you didn't come in just to watch me clean up everything I run into," I counter.

"What if I did?" he inquires.

My cheeks flush as I ask, "Huh?"

Real smooth there, Lucky, real smooth. I'm usually more articulate, but for some reason, he makes me stupid.

"I just thought you might like to grab a bite to eat?" He smiles as he asks.

"Um, with me? Are you sure you don't mean Crystal? I can go get her," I say as I put down the books and grab my phone to text her.

"No, Lucky. I meant you," he says, placing his hand over mine like he did the first day we met.

I swallow hard as I look into those blue eyes, "Like, now?"

"Yes, unless it doesn't work for you," he counters.

"Let me check and see if one of my sisters can take over for me," I say, removing my hand and phone from under his grip.

Me: Crystal, that hot guy is back. He wants to take me to lunch. Help.

Crystal: Oh Lucky, I told you he was eyeing you.

Me: Do you think I should go?

Crystal: If you want to. I think Coral and Wes are going out for lunch, if you don't want to be alone with him yet, have them tag along.

Me: That's a great idea. Can you ask her for me? If she says yes, have her come to the counter with you.

Crystal: See you in a minute. Try not to spill anything on his shoes this time.

I have to stop myself from laughing at that last sentence.

"Crystal's on her way. Did you want to look around while you wait?" I ask Felix.

"Only if you want to show me around. I know a little bit about this stuff but I'd like to know more." He smiles.

"If only I wasn't so clumsy I would jump at the chance. I'm still learning about some of the items we carry, but I know most of them by heart. That's what happens when you're a book nerd, I guess," I comment as my cheeks brighten since I just realized I called myself a nerd in front of this hottie.

He leans in a little closer toward me and whispers, "I'm a nerd, too."

"I don't believe it," I state.

He digs out his wallet and starts to rummage around. "Dang, I think I left my nerd card in my other wallet."

Felix smiles and so do I.

"Lucky, there you are! I thought you were getting ready

for lunch. Wes will be here to pick us up soon," Coral says as she gets to the counter, Crystal on her heels.

"Um, I forgot. Felix, here, asked me to lunch and I accepted. What if the four of us went together?" I ask hopefully, looking between my sister and Felix.

"I'm down," Felix replies.

Coral does a dramatic huff and breathes, "Fine."

I know that she's not really annoyed, she just put on that front to Felix. Before it can get any more awkward, the door chimes and Wes's happy whistle can be heard at the counter.

"Coral love, are you and Lucky ready?" he asks as he slips his arms around my sister's waist.

"We have an extra tagging along. This is Felix, Lucky's lunch date," she informs him, gesturing toward Felix standing in front of the counter.

Wes removes one hand from Coral and extends it toward Felix. "You're a brave man, taking Lucky out."

Felix accepts the hand and says as they shake, "What do you mean? You were already taking her to lunch. What makes me any different?"

"I'm used to her chaos, she means well, but if something bad is going to happen, it will happen to her," Wes says, returning his hand to my sister.

"Are we ready?" I ask, rocking on my heels. I'm a ball of nervous energy and say a silent prayer to anyone that will listen that this date will not be a complete disaster.

CHAPTER
Three

THE DATE - YEP, I REALLY DID THAT.

O f course, the restaurant that Coral picks is within walking distance. She just wants me to stumble or fall on my face in front of Felix.

"This place is my and Wes's favorite," Coral gushes as she holds on to Wes's arm.

"Have you ever been there?" Felix asks me.

"No, I don't get out much," I reply honestly.

"What? Why not?" he questions while he steadies me as I trip on the flat sidewalk.

"If you haven't noticed, I'm a girl with the name Lucky, except I'm anything but. Anything bad that can or will happen, seems to seek me out," I say.

"No one can be that unfortunate," he says in disbelief.

Just as he says that, a few birds fly overhead and one drops a present on my shoulder.

"Are you sure you want to have lunch with me?" I smile weakly.

"Yes, that isn't anything that can't be cleaned off in the restroom. Can't let this one thing stop us." He grins.

"Don't say she didn't warn you," Coral comments.

"It's not too late to change your mind," I tell him, "We can still turn around."

My stomach decides to growl and betray me.

"You're hungry, let's just go and see what happens," Felix says.

"It's your funeral," Coral whispers.

I only hope that Felix didn't hear that and it wasn't a prediction from my sister.

We walk in silence until Wes and Coral stop in front of a set of black doors.

I take a breath and turn to Felix, "Only if you're sure."

"I am," he says with a confident smile, taking my hand.

We walk into the dimly-lit restaurant, following my sister and Wes. They stop at the little hostess stand and get us a table.

Felix keeps a hold of my hand until we reach our seats and he pulls my chair out for me. I thank him as he pushes me toward the table and I knock over the water glass, soaking the table and my sister in the process.

"Ugh, Lucky," she sighs.

"I'm sorry," I start, as I use my napkin to sop up the cold liquid. Our waitress comes over to help.

"Save it," she says holding up a hand, "I know you didn't mean to and I'm not mad."

Wes stands and holds a hand out toward her to help her up.

"I'm going to the bathroom to see if I can dry some of this," she states as she heads deeper into the dark room.

"Should I go help her?" I ask Wes nervously.

"Nah, I know you mean well but it's best for you to stay seated," he replies.

"I feel bad. I didn't want to ruin your lunch date," I tell him.

"I've told you time and time again, it's not your fault you're so unlucky," Wes says, trying to ease my nerves.

"It's odd that your name is Lucky, but trouble seems to find you," Felix pipes up.

"I am the seventh daughter. My family named me Lucky because they believe that seven is a cursed number. My mom had hopes that it would change my fate, but as you can see, it didn't," I say.

"I told Coral, I thought that naming her Lucky is what condemned her," Wes shrugs.

"Well, I for one, think that you can change your fate. That nothing is written in stone," Felix states.

"I wish that were true," I mutter, as I unroll my silverware and my fork clatters to the floor. "See, bad luck."

My sister just returned and the fork almost hits her foot.

Felix places a hand on mine and I feel a warmth spreading through my body. *This is new,* I think as I glance at him, trying to see if there is any change in his expression. If he feels what I did, he doesn't show it.

"Don't worry, you can get a new one when we order," Felix smiles.

I smile at him before turning to my sister. "Can you show me the bathroom?"

"Of course. Gentlemen, if you'll excuse us for a moment," Coral tells the guys.

We both stand up and, of course, I bump the table and my chair falls to the floor. My cheeks flame as the others in the restaurant stare at me.

"Maybe I should go back to the store and stay in my bubble," I state.

"You will not," Coral says as she takes my arm. "Accidents happen, it's time you accept that."

She steers me toward the back and I head straight for the first open stall. I get the door locked before the tears start. How can I go out and face that sweet guy? What if he orders soup and I spill it on him? That would burn him; and a knife? There is no way I can be trusted with one of those.

Lost in my thoughts, I don't hear the knocks the first time, until my sister calls my name.

"You can't hide in there, Lucky," she calls from the other side of the door.

"No, but how am I supposed to do this? I'm going to hurt him or you. There is no way I can do that. Can you apologize to him for me? Maybe I can sneak out the back with minimal damage," I tell her as I dry up my tears.

"Come on, Luck, this guy really seems to like you. You've already spilled a potion on him at the store, do you really think that food is gonna be worse?" my sister asks.

"What if it's hot? I'll scald him," I remind her.

"So, no soup. You have to stop thinking about the worst that can happen. Sometimes, you just have to live in the moment," she tells me.

"But Mom, always—" I start but she cuts me off.

"Mom is not here. I've told you that she babied you too much for what might happen and that has you spooked. That is not a way to live. How are you ever going to have a life if you live in fear?" she asks.

"I've always just lived for the day, I've never thought about the future. With my luck, there is no telling when I'll trip and get hit by a truck," I remind her.

"And what a sad life to live. How are you ever going to find the love of your life, if you're tucked behind the counter of the family store?" Coral questions.

"Ha, I didn't know you were so funny, sis," I snark as I open the door. "How spotty am I?"

"Not too bad, are you still sneaking out and disappointing Felix, or are you coming back to lunch?" she asks.

"Only if you are okay with wearing your lunch," I tell her with a weak smile.

"As long as we match, I'll proudly walk back to the store." She laughs.

"Deal," I tell her as I give myself a once-over in the mirror.

My eyes are a little red but not too spotty, so back to the table, we go.

Coral takes the lead and makes sure that I don't hit anyone or anything. I'm grateful for this kindness.

When Felix notices that I'm back, he stands and pulls out my chair for me.

"Welcome back." He smiles as he pushes me closer to the table.

"Thanks, I just want a disclaimer. I'm not responsible for any accidents," I warn all of them.

"I think we will take our chances," Felix says to everyone at the table.

"Did the waitress already come by?" Coral asks.

"I already have a glass of wine headed your way," her boyfriend states.

"You know me so well." She smiles at him.

Is that what love looks like? That dreamy stare they have for each other?

"I just got water for you. I wasn't sure what you would like yet," Felix offers up.

"Water is perfect," I tell him. *There is no color to that,* I think to myself as I glance over the menu. Soup is out, I think that I'm safe with a salad but a steak really catches my eye.

"What are you thinking about for lunch?" Felix questions.

"I think a salad is a safe option," I tell him honestly.

"And that is what you really want?" Coral questions.

"No, but I'll make it work," I tell her.

Coral arches a brow at me but doesn't comment on it.

There is a lull in the conversation but everyone is just looking over the menu. The waitress comes back over and smiles widely at Felix. A little bit of anger rises in my chest, or is it jealousy? These are two new emotions for me.

"What can I get for you, good-looking?" she questioned Felix.

"Why don't you get their order first?" Felix says, pointing to Coral and Wes.

Wes doesn't give her a chance as he starts ordering, talking loudly since she didn't move.

I pretend to look over the menu, but I will order the salad.

"My sister will have the steak and side salad," Coral tells the waitress and this gets my attention.

I glance over at her and she just grins widely. How did she know that's what I wanted?

"Coral, me with a knife, that is just asking for trouble," I whisper.

"Don't worry, Wes will cut it up for you. Then you will not be near the knife and there's no chance of stabbing your date," she tells me.

"And Wes is okay with that?" I question.

"I am." He smiles.

Why are they doing this for me? How can I repay their kindness?

Coral hands me a napkin, "Don't go tearing up."

"It's really your fault," I remind her.

Once Felix orders, the waitress disappears again.

There's a lull in the conversation until, thankfully, Wes starts asking Felix some questions and that gets us all talking.

I mostly sit back and listen. My life is not much more than working or reading. And even reading is a challenge with my luck. I always get the worst paper cuts and pray I don't get blood on the book.

My side salad comes before all the other food and I mill around, not ready to eat it when I somehow launch a crouton from my plate and hit Felix in the forehead.

He doesn't get mad, he just laughs as he wipes away the ranch that is left as evidence.

"I think I'll just crawl in a hole and die now," I comment in a meek voice.

I glance to see that my sister and Wes are struggling to keep in their laughter.

"Lucky, I told you it doesn't bother me. Accidents happen," Felix states before taking a sip of his drink.

"I appreciate that, but it's normal for me. I just want to remind you that I am a walking bad-luck charm," I tell him.

The rest of the food arrives and true to my sister's word, Wes cuts up my steak without a complaint. I mouth a 'thank you' to him as he passes my food to Coral, who places it in front of me.

To my surprise, the rest of lunch goes smoothly. *Is this how normal people go through life?* This would be heaven for me.

The waitress comes back, "Any room for dessert?"

Felix looks at me and I shake my head no, which he replies to the waitress who seems to be ignoring the rest of us.

"I'll be right back with your bill," she huffs.

Wes leans over and whispers, "I think she wanted your number."

"Good for her," Felix smirks, "but I don't go on a date to get with other women."

"What a gentleman, you are," Coral states, as she elbows Wes.

"I'm a gentleman," Wes complains as he rubs his shoulder. "I've got the bill if you want to take Lucky back home."

"Are you sure?" Felix questions, "I don't mind paying for Lucky and me."

"Nah, you can cover it on the next date," Wes tells him.

"Thank you, Wes," I say as Felix offers me a hand.

"Are you ready?" he asked me.

"As I'll ever be," I say, letting out a long breath, and accepting his hand.

He does much like Coral did and leads me to the front door without one single unlucky thing. We are outside before Felix said anything.

"Are you okay, Lucky?" he asks with concern.

"Maybe? I'm just waiting for what is going to happen to me. It's been too long since anything bad has happened," I confess.

"Relax, if you don't want to date me, just tell me. You don't have to keep playing the bad luck game," he said.

"What? No, I'm not playing. I'm dead serious. You can ask anyone in my family. I am unlucky. If I didn't want to go, I would have said so," I promise before I trip on a rock on the sidewalk. "See, bad luck finds me."

He laughs, "This could happen to anyone."

"That's true, but it's usually me that it does," I tell him.

"Well, maybe I'm your lucky charm." He smiles.

"Oh?" I question, arching a brow.

"Yeah, if you believe in bad luck, why not good?" he questions.

"This is me," I tell him as we stop in front of the family shop.

He leans forward and kisses my cheek, and that same warmth spreads over my body.

"What time are you off?" he asks.

"Six, why?" I question.

"I'm coming back to pick you up for a proper date." He smiled before heading off.

I stand there in awe of this man that wants to date me, even though I'm a jinx.

Catnip & Hijinx

BY JUPITER DRESDEN

For Chelsey- you're a little bit of magic in my life I didn't know I needed.

CHAPTER
One

A sharp pain shoots through my head, waking me from my sleep. "Catnip!" I yell, swatting at the top of my head. "Leave me be or I'll turn you into a toad."

"I'd like to see you try," Catnip replies, as he claws the top of my head again.

"Worst cat ever," I moan as I sit up on the bed, my hand groping wildly at the nightstand in search of my glasses. "One day it *will* happen, You'll be a frog and not a fat cat."

"I'm only fat because you feed me all day long," Catnip retorts.

I find my glasses, putting them on to look at my familiar, "If you wouldn't give me those big eyes, I wouldn't give you my scraps."

I grant him a nice pet behind his ears.

"Enough about that, if you don't get moving you'll be late for work again," Catnip sounds annoyed.

"No, no way I set my alarm last night," I protest, grabbing my phone to check the time.

9:05 a.m. flashes on my phone.

"Why didn't you wake me sooner? Dang cat."

Frustrated, I toss the cover over him. I jump out of bed to

find something to wear. Thankfully, working at a coffee shop we don't have a uniform.

Just find something clean... clean, I know there's something lurking in this room.

After a few minutes of digging around, I find my favorite white 'meoow' shirt and denim leggings. Some mismatched socks will have to do until I get a day off. I paint my lips a bright pink, and swipe on some mascara and I'm done with my makeup. My hair looks like a rat's nest, so I brush out the bottom and throw a beanie on.

I rush out of the house without even looking in Catnip's direction as I snatch up the keys off the side table, slamming the door behind me. My steps cut short and I blow out a breath at the sight before me. My Chevy Malibu is parked in the driveway just like every other night. Only some asshat parked his stupid Ford truck behind me. I do my best to resist the urge to go back inside, grab a knife and slash all four of his honking tires. I don't have time to be as rude as Mr. Tiny Dick-and I'm late for work.

"Freaking Buttholes!" I scream to the sky, letting out my anger. I start the seven minute walk to work. One of the perks of small-town living—everything is close, though driving would be faster. I'm going to be late for work for sure. Rob's going to have my head, third time this week. So, I might have dragged my feet and took a couple minutes knowing the tongue lashing I'm about to receive.

As I walk into the coffee shop, Rob's voice doesn't assault my ears. All I hear is the buzz from everyone talking while waiting to order their drinks. The place is hopping as the line is almost out the door. Putting a hurry in my step, I head to the back to put my purse in my locker. I'll clock in later. Another thing I'll get scolded for, but these people need coffee. All Rob really does is yell at all of us, I don't know if I've ever heard him talk normally.

Lark smirks as she starts a smoothie in the blender. "Nice of you to finally join us, Chelsey."

"Oh, you know," I shrug as I count the till, "my alarm didn't go off, no clean clothes in sight, so I had to dig for some. And the topping of my day so far—some jerk parked behind my car, so I couldn't get out of my own driveway."

"Sounds like an awesome morning." Lark's cocky as she makes a cup of coffee.

"Catnip wasn't any help," I say as I slam the register closed. It's counted and ready to help people. "The butthole clawed my head. I'm sure he left marks and blood."

"I don't get why you keep that stupid thing around," she scoffs, as she pours the pink smoothie into the large cup next to the blender. "All cats are evil demons."

"More than you know," I mumble under my breath.

The rush lasts for over three hours, nonstop taking orders. Any free time is helping my co-workers make drinks, wiping down counters, tables, checking bathrooms. Most importantly, trying to remember to breathe.

We've never been this busy, ever.

"Lark, is there a festival going on or a holiday I've forgotten about?" I call over to her as I go out to the floor to wipe down a dirty table with a rag. Lark tries to answer me, but the door chimes, muffling her words.

As I reach the table, a stranger walks in, about six feet of a hunk of man. Someone I've never seen before in my year of living in this town where everyone knows everyone. Golden skin, blue jeans, and his bulging muscles are threatening to escape from the tight confines of his black t-shirt –that says Beast Mode. He's wearing a hat, but his hair looks to be short if not a buzz cut, I can't see any hair poking out in the front.

"Just take it off," I whisper under my breath, then drop my eyes and go back to cleaning the table.

Chelsey, get your head out of the clouds and get back to work.

Lark gasps behind me, making me spin around to see

what's happening. Mr. Sexy is in the middle of taking his shirt off. Holy crap, my magic slipped out again.

Catnip is going to kill me if I can't get it under control. I mumble for him to stop, hoping it will fix the problem and thankfully, it does. I sigh with relief as I go back to cleaning.

There's no way I can look at him after what I just made him do.

Chelsey, just keep your head down, your shift is almost over.

"Excuse me, miss," he says, his deep voice makes me almost jump out of my skin.

I can't look up, no I won't.

"How can I help you?" I ask as I move to the next dirty table without making eye contact.

"Looking at me would be a good start." Annoyance laces his voice.

"Sorry, just trying to get these tables clean before the next rush. But I will gladly assist you with any questions you might have."

I try to be as polite as possible. Not that I have a reason to be rude, just more embarrassed by my clumsy magic.

"I don't do this often. In fact, I feel a little strange saying this," he gulps. "But, I couldn't take my eyes off you from the moment I walked in here-"

My laughter cuts him off.

"That's real funny. Did Lark put you up to this, mister?" I finally lock eyes with his hunter-green eyes. "I'm just a walking jinx. Bad luck all the way."

I don't give him a chance to say another word and go to the back room, immediately pressing up against the wall and letting out a big breath. My heart flutters at the thought that anyone like him would even give me a second look.

After having my heart ripped out last year it's been closed for business. First loves are hard to get over. The move to Dread Ridge was a fresh start for me and Catnip.

Lark scurries in right behind me, she always has to know what's going on in my love life, or lack thereof.

"What is wrong with you?" she barks at me.

"Not sure what you mean."

I try to forget the oddness that just happened.

"Mr. Hotstuff was out there hitting on you and you blew him off like a tornado just came through the middle of town."

I snort. "That was the weirdest saying I've ever heard,"

"He's still out there. Bet you five dollars he waits for you to get off shift."

Lark winks and walks back out front. I hope not, but check anyway, peeking my head out. Sure enough, he still sits out front at one of the tables. He's facing right where he can see directly into the back. It's freaking me out a bit. Maybe I can duck out early today, probably a fat chance with how busy we've been. I'm hiding from him, I shouldn't be.

Just breathe. Breathe and get through your shift. Thirty minutes left.

I do everything I can to avoid the table the stranger is at. Lark even goes to see if he needs a refill or anything else.

"You never did answer me, Lark, is there something special going on this weekend? We just have so many new people in town for there not to be something happening here," I question her again as I make sure my area is stocked up for the next shift, filling syrup and cups up as well as stir sticks behind the counter.

"Boy, you don't pay attention to anything do you?"

Lark rolls her eyes before going to give Mr. Sexy another drink. This makes me wonder what I've missed that's right in front of my face. I look at the calendar to check the date, and see if there's anything special written on it. There's nothing other than what's low in-stock, so that's needed to be ordered for the next truck.

Rob pops in out of nowhere, "Chelsey, can you cover another shift? Tori called in sick."

"I wish I could, but you've been asking me a lot lately and my house is a mess. Plus, Catnip is almost to the point he doesn't know who I am anymore." I tell him as I plop the stir sticks into a cup next to the cappuccino machine.

Rob looks at me a bit puzzled. "Everyone has been passing that stomach bug around. I'm sorry. But I thought you wanted the overtime."

"I get it, but I just can't keep putting this stuff off." I look away, I can't lie to his face. "Plus, I've pulled three doubles this week alone. I just really can't cover tonight, too."

Rob nods and walks away, making me feel horrible for telling him no. I go over to my register and count it down without a word. The whole time I feel Mr. Sexy's eyes on me.

"Lark, you about ready to head out?" I question as I head back to the back room to hang up my apron.

"Yeah, I'm surprised Rob didn't talk you into staying."

She laughs as she hangs her apron up right next to where I had put mine.

I roll my eyes before I exit the back room. "Trust me, he tried. Do you want to come over tonight?"

Lark's close behind me. "You really don't know what's happening today, do you?"

"Yeah, drawing a blank."

"It's Dread Ridge's anniversary today. We've been a town for two hundred years today," she boasts as we clock out then proceed to walk out of the coffee shop.

I do everything I can not to look at the handsome stranger, but I can feel his eyes lingering on me.

I'm still lost to all this. "So, that means what to me?"

"They have a flea market, food trucks, and live music." Lark rolls her eyes. "You really didn't see all the signs posted around town?"

"Um, no." I shake my head. I must have been under a rock to have missed this. "Working all the extra shifts at the shop has really taken all my free time. All I've done is sleep and work. You don't even want to know what kind of underwear I have on…"

She stops at the corner and frowns at me. "You don't have any on, do you?"

"Anyways. Are you going to the flea market? It sounds like fun and Catnip could use the fresh air."

"Yeah, I'll be there around five," Lark says, but looks as if she's holding something back.

"But, what?" I poke at her, trying to see what she's hiding.

"I have a blind date," she says in a hushed tone.

I scoff. "Who set you up?"

"I'm not going to say. You'll only laugh."

"That pig Rob. He's been itching to get in your pants for months."

My smile fades at the thought she might be going on a date with him.

"In his dreams." She snickers. "No, it's a blind date. Rob did set it up, but it's like his nephew or something."

"I hope he's hotter than his uncle," I say, waiting for the little walk sign to tell me I can cross the street.

"At least younger, more hair on his head, less on his back, and a six pack would be nice."

The walk light blinks for me.

I call back, "Yeah, I hope he doesn't have a keg like Rob."

CHAPTER
Two

O f course, Catnip is waiting for me at the door when I get home. I give him a pet as I try to not bring up my slip at the coffee shop.

"So, are we having our normal boring, quiet night in?" Catnip asks, weaving in between my legs as I walk into the kitchen.

"Well," I start as I open the fridge, grabbing a pop. "Thought we could go downtown to the anniversary festival."

Catnip tilts his head, "What's the catch?"

"Yeah, you're going to have to wear the harness."

I wince at my own words, knowing how much he hates that thing.

"No deal." He shakes his tiny black head at me. "Too many people come up and pet me, saying how cute I am."

I tease him as I open the soda and take a swig. "You so know you are."

"Still a hard pass."

"Good thing I'm not really giving you a choice." I set my drink on the counter. "I'm going to change. So, hopefully, you'll be happier about going once I'm done. Plus, you need the fresh air."

"I'm a house cat now. House cats don't go outside," Catnip throws back at me as I walk out of the room.

———

The anniversary festival is like a flea market and carnival mixed together. I'm here for it. My first stop is the hot chocolate booth. Catnip meows at the smell, asking for his own. Everyone in town already finds me odd, so I like to give 'em what they want.

"Can I get two please?" I ask the lady manning the booth.

"Oh of course, dear." She smiles as she pours out two cups. "One for you and one for your boyfriend?"

She hands me the cups.

"No, ma'am, for me and my cat. He likes all human stuff, so I treat him when he's good on his leash."

"You kids these days. I don't get you," she says as she shakes her head. "It will be four dollars for the cocoa."

"Yes, ma'am." I hand her a five. "Just keep the change and thank you for the drinks."

Catnip pulls me, but I'm not sure where he's taking me. I thought he wanted this drink. It's easier to just follow. Being seen yelling at a cat on a leash is not a good look.

"So, you already want to sit?" I ask him as he hops up on a bench.

'Meow'

"As you wish." I set his hot chocolate down and open the lid. Catnip pops his head right in the cup, licking it up. I take a swig of mine, it's not very hot. Lukewarm at the most—which is good, so he doesn't burn his little tongue.

"Well, well, what are the chances I'd run into you here?" a familiar voice comes from behind me, freezing me in my tracks. "So, you're going to pretend you don't hear me?"

If I don't make a move maybe he'll leave. But he taps my shoulder this time, so I suck it up and turn to the man from the shop.

"I'm trying to make sure my cat doesn't drown himself in his hot chocolate. Is that okay?" I mutter, annoyed that he's found me so fast.

"That's a new one for me. I don't think I've ever seen anything like that before." He chuckles.

"Catnip is one of a kind," I say as I take another sip of my drink.

"That's something I can most definitely see." He leans down, giving Catnip a stroke down his back. "So, you want to walk around with me and show me what this is all about?"

"Oh, I would love to, but my date might get jealous." I bat my eyes at him as I pick Catnip up, he's still licking his chops from the hot cocoa. "He has claws."

"Well he doesn't look too danger—"

Catnip cuts him off with a hiss and swipes at him.

"Oh, you were about to say what?" I smirk as I pick up the cup from the bench. "So, I guess you got your answer."

With that, Catnip and I go to find a trash can and then off to see what else this place has to offer.

After looking at about three booths selling pretty much the same thing: bath salts, lotions, and soaps, we come to one that catches my eye. This is something I've never seen in Dread Ridge, it looks to be an apothecary shop. Candles adorn the tables, along with little bottles full of herbs and salts among other earthly things.

Catnip meows at me, probably telling me to leave. The witch in me is drawn into all this, though. I don't heed his warning and step into the little shop to take a closer look. A creepy guy comes out from behind the curtain. His long, greasy, brown hair looks like he hasn't washed it in days. The faint smell of Cheetos and cheap beer linger on his breath as he yawns next to me.

"Can I help you find anything, ma'am?"

"Just looking." I smile. "You don't see this kind of stuff in town."

"I'm a traveler. I do shows all over the states. Welp, let me know if you see anything you like."

I nod and turn back to all the little goodies. There's a bunch of different crystals, an unknown force guides my hand towards the selenite.

What is wrong with me?

"Catnip, something is wrong," I breathe, setting him down. "Go find Lark."

At this point, I can hardly move. My body's frozen, breathing is becoming difficult. Hopefully, Catnip gets help fast. A laugh comes from beside me. The vendor is standing next to me, breathing his horrid breath on me again.

"Well, my dear, the reason you've never seen a shop like this is I'm a witch hunter," he explains as he walks to the other side of me. "To everyone else this all looks like junk. But to witches it's an apothecary shop. To trap a witch you have to use a bit of magic."

I want to scream at the hypocrite, using magic to lure me in. Catnip warned me against people like this, but I thought it was a myth. Nowadays, why would people want to hurt us? Most don't even believe in witches.

"Why?" I squeak out.

He laughs again. "You ask why? Maybe because people like you killed my family. My mother and father are gone because of witches."

"Not me," I peep, tears forming from the pain of trying to keep air flowing through my body.

"You horrid creatures are all the same," he hisses, putting his arms around my waist. "Time to put you in the van and see if I can find any more like you in this town."

"No more."

He starts to drag me toward the back. "Ha, you think I'd

ever believe you. You probably have a coven here you're trying to hide.".

I will myself to scream, kick, or bite him, but nothing happens. Whatever he's done to me is really strong, could he have used magic on me? My fate is resting on Catnip, it feels like eternity waiting for him to reappear with someone, anyone.

"Oh my dear girl, I wonder what's going on in that pretty little head of yours."

He sneers as he pulls me behind the curtain. A tear falls down my cheek as I feel all is lost. Catnip never steered me wrong, I'm just hard headed and thought I knew better. He is teaching me for a reason, if I get out of this, I'll listen to him 99% of the time.

He opens the side of the van door, and throws me in. I crash onto my shoulder, pain radiating down my arm. I'm not sure how I'm still breathing at this point. My legs are pushed in, it feels like he ties them then my hands together. Once done, the van door slowly starts to creak closed.

Darkness creeps at the edges of my vision as I let myself give in.

Catnip will have to find a new witch to teach. Surely, he'll do better with them.

Eventually, everything goes black.

CHAPTER
Three

I wake up, gasping for air. The hold on my body is quickly breaking. My arms and legs are still bound, as I stretch out.

Crap, how am I still in this van?

It's hot, sticky, and the smell here is horrible, like gasoline mixed with throw up. Once I'm able to move around more I sit up. That stupid guy didn't tie my hands up very well. He must have thought I'd be frozen a lot longer than I was.

Stupid idiot.

That horrible smelly man did know how to tie a knot on my feet, it feels like an eternity trying to get my legs free. Plus, will I be able to even get out of this rust-bucket or did he make it witch-proof, too?

Freedom at last. Kinda.

The back doors are the first ones I go for. No dice, there are no handles for me to even try.

That bastard.

I'm afraid to try the front, what if he sees me? Then again, I've got to get out of this pit. I sneak to the passenger window facing where he'd be tending his booth. I don't see him right offhand, maybe he's helping someone in his stupid fake, witch-catching booth. With that, I move over to the driver's side. I click unlock and nothing. Dread fills my stomach.

"Just unlock," I blurt out.

The lock mechanism makes a popping sound, so I try again. The door swings open, with a horrible squeaking sound. I get out of the vehicle in a hurry, looking both ways to see if anyone's there. Thankfully, Cheeto-and-beer breath hasn't made an appearance.

Catnip went to get help, but not being able to talk to anyone they might have thought he had gotten free from me. At least he'll be safe, as long as he found Lark. Hopefully, I can find them quickly and get lost in the crowd. This asshole will not get a second chance to snatch me.

After another glance around, I make my break for it. My legs don't want to run, though, and even walking is harder than expected. But I won't let it stop me. I lift my heavy legs one at a time. I make some progress, I've passed two tents, ducking in a booth when I hear the van door creak open.

Thankfully, the lady running this one is helping someone, so she doesn't freak out at me coming in from the back. I pretend to be interested in her handmade cookies, slipping my hand in my pocket. I pull a five out, taking the peanut butter cookies, so maybe she won't wonder why I look a mess.

She smiles at me and I exit the booth. Cheeto Man lets out a yell. Or at least I think it's him. My legs are working better and I'm able to move faster. An arm slips into mine, making me jump.

"Just keep walking," Mr. Sexy says.

"What are you doing?" I mumble, trying to get my arm free but he holds firm.

He laughs. "Trying to help you, but if you don't want it, I can take you back to the carny reject."

"Would you like to tie me back up, too?" I stop dead in my tracks.

His right eyebrow raises "I mean, is that an offer?".

"Heck no!" I try to pull away from him and almost fall. My legs need the support, trying to recuperate. "I'm too weak to walk on my own, so you're lucky to even be touching me."

"Wow, you are snippy."

"You try being drugged and then hog tied by a carny-looking guy." I huff as I try to let go of him again.

He tugs me closer. "Just keep hold of me until we're far from him, Chelsey."

"My legs are waking up, so you don't need to use a Kung fu grip on me. Plus, I have made good distance. I really need to find Catnip. If he's lost I just don't know what I'd do."

Mr. Sexy laughs. "Cats always find their way home. You need to rest."

He isn't wrong, but there's no way I'm going to let him anywhere near my home.

Lark. I need to find Lark.

He motions to a bench close by. "Why don't you just sit down for a moment? Catch your breath."

"Fine, if only to get your sweating hands off me," I grumble as I plop my butt on the semi-cool cement. "But riddle me this, how did you know my name?"

"Ummm. Yeah, you do wear name tags at your work. I make a habit out of reading them."

He seems to be getting tired of my sass, but Catnip said to keep my guard up at all times. So, to me, that means to be harsh, push people away.

"Fine, one point for you," I say, eyeballing him. "But why are you following me? You seemed to be there right when I needed help. You've just been popping up everywhere. Kinda creepy if I do say so."

"I'm in town on business. You just happen to be everywhere I'm going." He lets out a laugh. "But if you don't want anything from me, I'll leave."

"Oh, wow did I hurt your widdle heart?" I glare at him, even though I should be nicer since he did just help me. "I thank you for your help, enjoy your time in Dread Ridge."

I bid him farewell as I try to stand, falling back down onto the bench. My legs felt fine, then weak again.

How can he hate magic so much, but be able to use it? Something rubs up against my leg, making me jump. A meow comes from under the bench, I have a gut feeling it's Catnip.

I glance under the seat. "Did you find me, Catnip?"

"He's not the only one." Lark's voice sounds out behind me. "But it looks like you found someone to keep you company."

"I was just leaving," Mr. Sexy rumbles out.

Lark sits down next to me. "But Catnip and I just showed up."

"What happened to your blind date?" I turn to her, as Catnip jumps in my lap.

"No show. But it looks to me like you have one," Lark says with a nod and a wink.

"Who him? I don't even know his name."

I let out a cackle as I love on Catnip. So glad he's safe.

"Van," he mutters.

"What about a van?" Lark looks at him.

I give him a kick, she doesn't need to know about the carny van.

He steps out of my leg range. "My *name* is Van."

"Well, nice to meet you. Ches, must really like you if she's already kicking you. That's normally left for the third date." She snorts.

"Does she have a lot of third dates?"

"If she could ever get a first one maybe."

"I am sitting right here." Catnip can tell I'm pissed and

hops off my lap. "I'm getting food and heading home. You two can go on a date."

"Yeah, I'm all dated out for the night," Lark says. "I might do the same as you."

"I never agreed to a date anyway." Van doesn't seem happy with our conversation. "I'm just here to see what this town has to offer while on business. I bid you goodnight, ladies."

Once Van is gone, Lark jumps down my throat. "Why do you always do that? He was so into you,"

"I don't need a man to be happy. The only man I need is Catnip. He's plenty to handle." I giggle, petting him.

"Fine but Mister Right is going to slip right through your fingers and you'll never know.

"Did you see any good food trucks now that I have no butt left?" I tease.

Lark stands, extending her hand to me. "Why yes, let's go get our grub on."

Once Catnip and I get home, the first thing he does is curl up in a ball and fall asleep. Now I'm left to my thoughts as I sit next to Catnip petting him and overthinking all the events that happened today. If that Carny has followed me home, he'll get a taste of my magic. This time, I'll be ready for the jerk.

I wake up to the sound of the doorbell, looking down at my phone, it's 9 a.m.

Who the heck is here so early?

The bell rings again, my heart stops for a moment, what if he's found me? I'm not ready to fight him. Heck, I don't want to fight anyone.

"I'm coming, I'm coming," I yell as the doorbell rings nonstop.

Finally, I open it to find Van standing there. He looks me up and down with a grin.

"Good morning, Chelsey."

"Ummm…" I'm speechless, pure shock. "How, just how, do you know where I live?"

"I told you, I had business in town." His voice turns stern.

The End.

Love Spells and Whisker Whispers

BY: M. CALDER

For Wren, my favorite little witch–I mean teenager–who is always my toughest critic and my biggest fan.

CHAPTER
One

I t's just another day in Stardust Hallow with two of my sisters trying to shove a nasty potion down my throat. This time, it's to regrow my eyebrows, ones I somehow burned off last night when trying to get dinner to boil. I really need to stop using magic to cook, or for anything really. As the youngest of seven girls, my uselessness with magic is such an embarrassment to our parents.

"Come on, Bellatrix," my sister, Celestia, urges. "It's better than looking like you're a surprised potato all the time. Especially when you're at work with Thadeus."

Thadeus. The gorgeous wizard I work with every single day at Midnight Brews, the local coffee shop. He's so dreamy, with his dark hair, light brown eyes, and jawline that could crack walnuts. Every time I see him lift a heavy tray of drinks to bring to a table, I have to wipe the drool from my mouth.

"Are you listening to us?" Sable shouts. She's another one of my sisters, older by one year, but she acts like she's my mother.

I tear my thoughts away from Thadeus and look at her blankly, "What?"

"Ugh, you are such a jerk, Bella. Would you just drink the damn thing? I have to go meet mom at the dress shop." Celestia loses her patience, which isn't hard since she's not the sweetest of us girls. She's right smack in the middle of ages and is marrying her one true love, Finnigan, in a few months. Well, technically it's called a handfasting, but I like human words better.

Taking the cup from her, I plug my nose and down it, trying to miss my tongue so I don't get so much taste. It doesn't work and I gag. "Ew, this is nastier than the one yesterday. Can't you put some elderberry juice in it or something to mask the flavor?"

Celestia lets loose a heavy sigh, which almost comes out like a growl, while Sable titters in the background. "This is why you're such a screwup with magic, Bellatrix. You should know adding extra ingredients will mess it up."

I do know, but I'm done defending myself to everyone around me. No matter how well I follow the instructions, my magic just does not go right all the time. Okay, most of the time, if I'm being honest. "Sorry," I apologize, which seems to be all I do anymore. "I'm going to go put on some makeup and maybe draw some eyebrows in case this doesn't work. You go and have fun picking out a dress. I know whatever you choose, Finnigan is going to love it."

This changes her mood—she eats up compliments—and her tone changes to excitement. "Do you really think so?" I nod and she hugs me, kissing me on the cheek. "This is why you're my favorite sister. I can't wait to find the perfect dress. I just know it will call to me."

"It will. Now go. I'll be okay, even if the potion doesn't work." She doesn't hesitate, and I call to her retreating back, "Have fun, Celestia."

Sable is next to leave, stating she has to go to work down at the bookstore and I head upstairs to put my makeup on and check my eyebrows. I know my sister doesn't really have to work for a couple more hours, but she's using it as an excuse to see Cedric. They've been dating on and off for a year, but our parents don't exactly approve of him. He's a lower-level wizard and to them, not good enough for their daughter. The fun of being the children of a highly respected family, with a father as the High Priest. One would think us all, being adults, would have negated their control over us, but that's not how it works in this coven. Unmarried witches have to live with their parents until they marry, something I don't think I have a chance of.

I roll my eyes thinking about it... OUCH! I stabbed my eyeball with the eyeliner. "Get it together Bella," I mutter to myself, wiping the tears away and trying to stop the black from running down my cheek.

Blinking hard, I finally have my eyesight back and I gasp as I spot my face in the mirror. The spell worked. A little too well.

I have caterpillars for eyebrows.

Big, fluffy, ridiculously hairy brows across my forehead.

"Goddess, no!" I panic, looking for the tweezers. Or maybe a hedge trimmer.

I find the wax my sisters use all the time. They're so into their beauty, of course they do. Me, I haven't used it before but it can't be that hard, right?

For most people, no. For me? Well, I'll just say I did not get the right temperature and now have red burn marks around my crooked eyebrows. Fuck my life.

"My hat!" I exclaim, realizing I can just wear my pointy hat and push it low on my head. It will keep my bangs down to cover the horror of what has happened to me. Seriously, I would have been better off going sans eyebrows or drawing them on like the old witch down the street does. Serenity is a bit eccentric, constantly wearing brightly colored robes for handfastings—claiming celebrations are colorful—and her makeup is like how they wore it in a bad 80s sitcom.

Running to my room, I quickly change into my uniform and grab my hat, setting it on my head. I have to tug hard to get it to sit right, but at least my forehead nightmare is covered. With one last look in the mirror, I race out of the house and get on my bike to try to make it to work on time.

CHAPTER

Two

T hadeus looks so sexy. I swear that man makes the simple white polo shirt and black dress pants look like he's at a high-end fashion shoot. Me, I look like a slob. My shirt is stained beyond saving and my black skirt keeps turning around to the seams in the middle. At least my bright blue apron covers the front of it. I can't exactly adjust my skirt all day when my hands are constantly full, with coffee cups and plates of desserts.

"It sure is busy today," he says to me on a trip back to grab the pumpkin spice latte I just made for his table. "Nice hat, by the way. It looks good on you."

"Um, yeah, thanks," I squeak, chiding myself for how dorky I am in his presence. "Looks like we won't get our break anytime soon." My stomach chooses that moment to grumble. I hadn't eaten breakfast with the whole eyebrow issue this morning and am cursing my sisters. Well, not really cursing, because it will probably come back to me with my wonky magic.

He gives me a panty-melting grin and I try to keep myself from swooning. "I only have this one table left to serve, then you can take a quick break. The customers should be fine."

"That would be great," I say, a little too enthusiastically. I swear, I sound like either a complete dork or a cheerleader at a pep rally whenever we work together. There's no in-between for me when it comes to Thadeus.

Hiding my embarrassment, I hurry to get the order filled. As klutzy as I am, somehow, I can fill the orders of hot beverages—yes, hot—without burning myself. As long as I don't use my magic at work, I'm fine.

"Two mocha lattes, a black coffee, and three apple spice donuts," I repeat the order as I load up the tray for him to take.

"Thank you, Bellatrix." He's one of the few people who uses my full name, and I don't mind it at all when he winks at me. "You go ahead and I'll hold the fort down."

I don't hesitate, grabbing a donut and a chocolate croissant, and go out the back door into the alley. Most people think of alleys as dirty and smelly, but not in this town. Stardust Hallow is a town full of witches and wizards. Not even one wrapper will stay on the street, disappearing as soon as it hits the ground. I love my town. If only I could not be such a screw up when it comes to magic.

Sitting at the little bistro set outside the back door, I shove the donut in my mouth first and moan. Midnight Brew really does have the best pastries in town, not that we have any competition or that I've been anywhere else to compare it to. With me being so glitchy, my parents always leave me home when they travel to other covens for business.

What I wouldn't give to be able to see the world in more than just online pictures and videos. Yes, the view here is phenomenal, tucked into a valley with green rolling hills all around, along with a crystal-clear creek running through the center of town. Stardust Hallow was built around the creek, with one small, decorative bridge crossing over it. There aren't any cars here since all witches can teleport to anywhere else. Except me, of course. My teachers were afraid

I'd end up on another planet if I tried again after the incident.

What incident?

Well, I sort of teleported to a place I shouldn't have and caused a little mishap. I was supposed to just go from one side of the grassy field to the other, only a few feet. I guess I overestimated my jump and landed in the potions room. On the shelf where all the ingredients are stored. And I didn't land lightly, crashing on top of it and smashing all the bottles. Mr. Mystere rushed to help me and turned purple. Not mad purple, but as in, his skin was stained purple for a week. He looked like a grape with his big, round belly, which he didn't find funny at all when I told him.

After that, they stopped trying to teach me the more dangerous things and I haven't tried since. Though, what I wouldn't give to be able to get out of this place and travel, even for just a day. Ireland is my home, but I know there's more out there, like the Greek statues and Roman buildings. And what I wouldn't give to take an underground train in London.

My thoughts are interrupted by what sounds like a cat meowing. I pause to see if I can hear it again, and sure enough, there it is. "Hello little kitty," I coo, trying to get it to come out.

It works, and this little black furball prances up to me, rubbing itself on my leg and purring. "Oh, you are so sweet!" I exclaim, reaching down to scratch its head. It's friendly and I try to pick it up, knocking my hat off in the process.

Whatever. It's not like this cat will judge me for looking so horrible. Animals just like love and attention, something I have five more minutes to give. It blinks at me and lets out a mewl which I can't interpret. "Are you lost, little one?" I ask and he jumps into my lap, making itself quite comfortable.

As it moves around, I see it's a male. He doesn't stop with the moving, standing so his front legs are on my breastbone and his face is right in mine. "You must be hungry," I speak to him like he's a baby. "I can get you some milk. I don't think donuts or coffee are good for cats. Not that I'd know since my parents refuse to let me have one." I sigh, thinking of everything I'm not allowed to own because of my mishaps in the past. I swear, it wasn't my fault the mice escaped their cage and disappeared into the walls. I shut their door, just forgot to lock it.

I swear I see the cat nod its head. "No, it has to be my imagination. Cats can't understand people."

"They can when they are familiars or aren't really cats at all," the cat says and I jump out of my chair, sending him flying. He lands on his four paws and lets out what I can only describe as a huff. "It's a good thing I'm quick on my feet. At least this body has great reflexes."

My head swims and blackness clouds my vision. I'm not able to sit before everything goes dark.

CHAPTER
Three

I wake up to a rough tongue on my face, and not for the first time in my life. Well, something wet on my face, not the licking. My eyes flutter open and I see big, golden eyes staring at me. "Ow," I groan as the pain in my head hits me, though I'm used to pain by now.

"You hit your head pretty hard," the cat says.

"I must have if I'm hearing a cat speak."

He snorts and blinks at me with those big, judgy eyes. Maybe he's not judging me, but I feel like he is. Everyone does. "I think it was my speaking that made you faint. I'd say I'm sorry, but I'm not. I need your help." He stares at me, and I'm not sure what to say.

I blink at him, wondering if my sister's concoction has caused hallucinations as a side effect. The cat seems to read my mind. "No, this is real. Though I didn't think you hit your forehead on the table so hard to have such a large red mark on it. I would assume you look worse on the back of your head from when you hit the ground. I can't smell any blood, but I should check to make sure. Can you sit up?"

"I—I don't think so, buddy. I need to get back to work. I've worked through worse injuries." It's sad but so, so true.

"Oliver."

"What?"

"My name is not Buddy, it's Oliver. And who might you be?" This Oliver cat is partially rude and partially polite. I'm not sure how to digest everything going on.

"Bellatrix, but my friends call me Bella. Wait, why am I still talking to a cat? I have to get back in before I get fired. I can't leave Thadeus all alone…" I ramble as I stand, swaying a little as dizziness hits me. At least the good news is that I can function better dizzy than most people, maybe even better than being clear-headed.

There's no way I'm going to stay out here with this talking creature. As I enter the door, I hear him say, "I'll be waiting for you, Bella."

"Not my friend," I grumble when I enter the shop. I see Thadeus is standing at the coffee bar and not doing much of anything. The crowd thinned while I was gone for… twenty minutes! "I'm so sorry, Thadeus. I hit my head, and it took me a bit for my brain to stop twirling."

Thadeus turns around with a smile on his face, that adorably friendly one where the dimples pop out, but it drops as soon as he takes me in. "Bella, your forehead! You need to get some ice on that. I could do a healing spell if you want. I'm not the greatest at it, but at least it will bring down some of the redness." He moves closer to me, and I can smell his spicy aftershave. It takes a lot for me to not start sniffing him like a dog. "Wow, I've never seen anyone with such a bright red mark after hitting their head. It must hurt so much. Let me get you healed."

I don't tell him the red is from waxing. Really, I don't tell him anything at all. I just stand there in awe, drinking in his sexiness while his hand hovers over my forehead. Feeling the warmth of his magic fills me with a sense of longing, a yearning for him to actually touch me. My embarrassment is long gone since I'm too busy basking in his attention.

I find Thadeu... muscle-bui... forehead ... as I thought at hea... me. "Oh, I found your ... after my break, but I guess y... didn't realize how fast the time we...

Hesitantly, I take it from his outstre... to touch those big, strong hands of his. I sw... person I've ever met who is perfect in every... you," I respond, plopping it on my head and pulling... "I really appreciate it. You have another hour, right?" As... stumbling through awkward conversation, I'm scanning for the black cat. So far, I can't see him.

"Yep. That's as long as Trina shows up on time." He lets out a sigh and rolls his eyes. "I swear that girl will be late to her own funeral."

I let out a not so endearing snort and my face flushes. "She's young. You know how teenagers are, thinking everything is more important than work," I say, as if I'm so much older and wiser at twenty years old.

CHAPTER THREE

When he's done, I thank him and tell him to go... and push when he protests. "I'll be fine. You're so goo... healing, Thad, and I'm so used to injuries, it's nothin... Now go."

With a salute, he does as I ask, and I'm left alone with my thoughts. Apparently, a cat named Oliver talked to me and I have no idea where he came from or how he can talk. I mean, I magical community and all things considered, it shouldn't be so unusual, but it is.

I'm caught between wanting to find out why and how, and fear keeping me from doing any of that. It's not like I can protect myself if he's some evil spirit meant to harm me. I don't know. The whole situation is worse than anything I've experienced so far in my life, and that's saying a lot. Not even the purple Mr. Mystere was as bad as this is. At least then, something unexpected had been bound to happen, with all the powerful ingredients mixing together like they did. But this, this is freaky.

Oliver did say he needs help, though I have no idea how an unworthy, unsuccessful witch like me can help him. I can't even help myself. Before I can decide on what to do, my shift replacement pops in, making me jump and knock over the cream container. "Goddess, Waverly! You scared me!"

She grabs some rags and tosses them to me. "It's not like you couldn't hear my heels," she answers dryly. "You really need to pay more attention. If you did, you wouldn't be such a screwup." She glances at me and exclaims, "What the heck happened to your forehead?"

"Just hit it on the table outside," I lie.

Rolling her eyes, she huffs, "You'll never change, Bella-trix." With that, she turns her back on me and puts on her apron.

I bite my tongue and finish cleaning up my mess, something I'm very good at. Waverly, like most of the other women in Stardust Hallow, doesn't have any qualms about showing

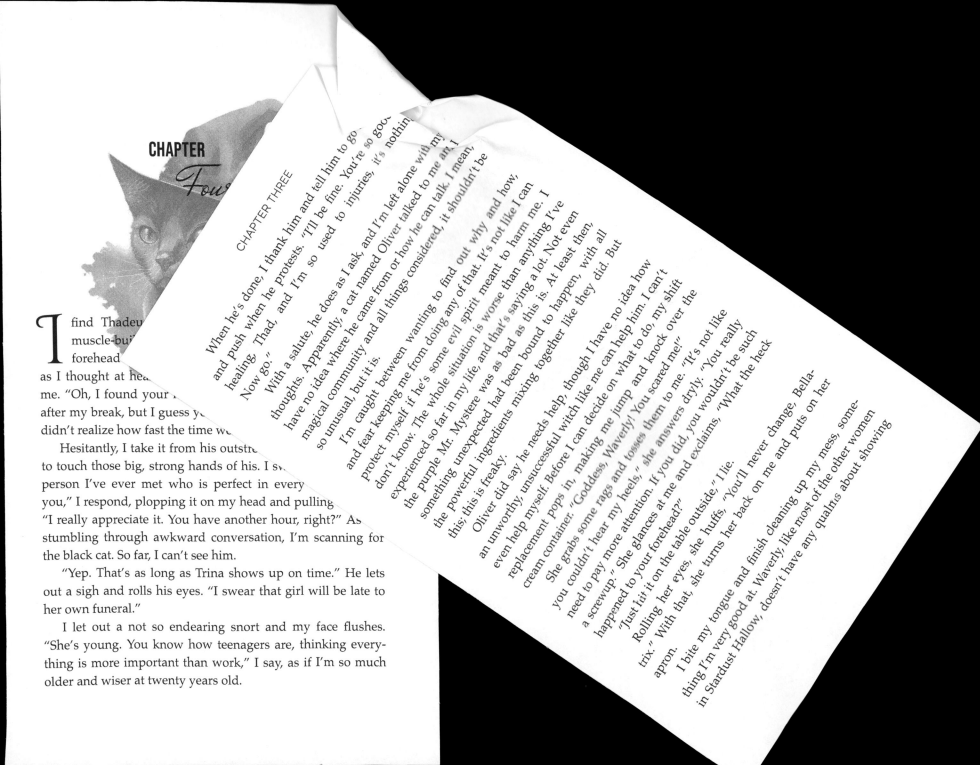

"This is true. I don't think I would care as much if it weren't for me needing to pay for university."

"Only another year and you'll be working for the council, doing great things for our coven." I try not to focus on the fact that I have zero future in this town, having been denied entrance to our magical university.

"You're so kind, Bella. Really, you're a good person."

Kind, but not good enough for him. Or anyone. "Thanks. So are you." I stand there awkwardly, twisting my hands together in the following silence. "Well," I point over my shoulder, "I'm going to get going. Things to do and people to see." I don't, but he doesn't need to know that.

"Yeah, I have to get back in before Waverly bites my head off."

I would have thought he would be more excited to work alongside his girlfriend. Trouble in paradise? I want to dig deeper and get all the juicy gossip on their relationship, but he gathers up his things and goes back inside before I can open my mouth, giving me a wave over his shoulder.

Sighing, I stand there and try to think if my sister, Elara, said anything. She's the town gossip, to put it mildly. Nothing happens in Stardust Hallow without her knowledge. The benefit of being able to read the future and minds, a skill I clearly didn't get. I would have known if she said anything, since I miss nothing about Thadeus in conversations. I shrug, thinking I might have to visit her, and wondering if it's worth it. She doesn't hate me, but she can be just as mean as Waverly and her group of friends. Honestly, Elara has always been just like my enemy, cruel and unforgiving to even her own sister.

"If you're done drooling over Mister Gym Rat, we can talk about how you're going to help me," Oliver says, appearing from behind a large potted plant.

I jump and let out a screech. "Warn a girl, buddy."

"It's Oliver, and it's not my fault you're so jumpy. You

really need to make yourself a nice relaxation potion. I wouldn't want you to hit your head again. Oh, wait, you already did twice."

Annoyed with his attitude, I retort, "You know, for someone who wants help, you're certainly not making your case by insulting me."

"Ah, the young witch has a backbone. Nice to see you can give it right back." I swear he grins at me as the amusement rings through his words. "Anyway, is there somewhere we can go to sit down and talk? Maybe the park? It's a long story and I'm sure you'll be more comfortable anywhere other than this alley. I'd rather not be interrupted."

"Okay. Most of the townsfolk are working, so it will be empty," I agree, smacking my forehead when I realize I agreed to something I didn't want to do. "Ouch," I groan as my not yet fully healed forehead stings.

Oliver lets out a chuff, which I assume is a laugh. Frustrated, I snap, "I would be nice if you wouldn't laugh at me. I get enough crap from everyone else and don't need a cat doing the same."

"Sorry, Bella. I've had a tough few months and I shouldn't take it out on the only person helping me." He truly sounds sorry.

"Apology accepted," I wave my hand as if it's nothing. I look at my bike and back at him. The park is a little far and, with as much attention as I get, walking and talking to a cat is way too much for my liking. It would get back to my parents, and it might be the last straw for them. "Can I pick you up and put you in my basket? I have a change of clothes in there so you could hide in them." I actually have three, but who's counting? They're needed just in case I spill something on whatever I'm wearing. I already get enough crap without having to get through a day with stains or burns on my clothes. Maybe I suck at magic, but I don't have to look like a vagabond while out and about.

"Sure," he replies, and I pick him up and carefully set him in the bike's basket. Rearranging the clothes to hide him, I climb on my bike and start pedaling. The slight breeze ruffles my hair and it feels good, blowing away all my stress from the day. Despite the rough morning, I'm determined to make the rest of the day good.

We pass by shops and I weave through people, weaving around the few witches out and about. No one notices the cat who is sitting in the basket talking to me. Oliver is actually being nice, asking me about myself and this time not judging me for my answers.

I hit the path inside the sprawling park, rife with trees, bushes, and an array of flowers in every color of the rainbow. It's beautiful and gives me a sense of peace, hidden from the judging eyes which always follow me everywhere I go. This park is my only sanctuary from my family and the townsfolk who always put me down. I have explored every inch of it and know the perfect spot where no one ever goes.

Stopping at the end of a main trail, I get off my bike and put the kickstand down. There's no one around, so I unbundle Oliver and pick him up. "Do you want me to carry you? It's a very short hike to the only spot I know we won't be interrupted."

"You can hold me. I think I'm still shaking from the harrowing ride here. I've never ridden in a bike basket and the experience has rattled me a bit."

I giggle and pick him up, his fur so soft against my bare arms. Walking doesn't take long at all. He's not heavy or anything and we make fast time getting to the tree-enclosed hiding spot. I set him down on the grass where he stretches out his body and makes himself comfortable. "So, what is it you want me to know about you, and why do you think I'm the best person for the job?"

CHAPTER
Five

Oliver starts his tale, "I'm not actually a cat. I'm a wizard who was cursed by someone after I hurt a witch in my coven. A powerful witch forced me into this body and sent me away." He looks down at his paw and shakes his little head, such a human gesture that I believe him. "I never intended to hurt her, the friend. You see, our families were close, and they basically forced us on each other. I always saw her as a friend, nothing more, but she felt differently, something I wish I had seen earlier. Time went by and suddenly our families started planning our handfasting. By the time I realized what was happening and found the courage to stop it, it was too close to the day. I told her I didn't love her like she deserved, but it didn't matter to her. She claimed I would learn to love her and we would be happy, that her love for me would be enough..." He trailed off and I waited for the rest.

"I'm not the kind of man who wants to hurt people. I swear, Bella, I'm kind and have a big heart. Maybe it's my heart which got me into this mess, but it wasn't my intention. I panicked when she wouldn't let me go, more for her than for myself. I could live with whatever came my way and take care of her as a friend, but I knew she deserved better. Everyone deserves their soulmate, don't you think?"

"I do," I agreed, saddened by his plight. If I were in the woman's shoes, I would have wanted to be told the truth. I'll be a spinster because no one is capable of loving a witch like me, clumsy and useless.

"I ran. Disappeared into the woods where I came across an old, empty house. At least, I thought it was empty. After a few days of sleeping on the dusty couch, I was woken up by a hag, one I found out after was the great aunt of my friend. The reason she was gone was because she was attending our handfasting, only to discover I ran away and left her family heartbroken. She told me I needed to learn my lesson and cursed me to this body until I find love. An impossible task because who could love an animal as anything more than a pet? Could you imagine the embarrassment? No one would be willing to truly get to know me as a person."

"I understand," I said heavily, wiping away a stray tear. "No one will get past my lack of magical abilities to know my heart."

Oliver climbed onto my lap and put his paws on my chest, looking me in the eye, "You will find someone. Mister Gym Rat was very nice to you. If he is, there must be something wonderful about you."

I let out a short, humorless laugh. "No, he has many girl-friends and is just a nice guy. He'll never be more than friendly with me."

"You're worth more, Bella. We all are. Yes, you seem to be quite accident prone, but considering you took me, a strange talking cat, seriously and wanted to help? Well, I think it shows what a good heart you have. You just need the right man to see it."

I shift uncomfortably with a compliment, something I never receive from anyone, and ask him more about his predicament. "I'm not sure how I can help you. My magic never works right, so I certainly couldn't reverse it. I know curses and they are unbreakable unless you fulfill them."

Getting off me, he sat next to me and leaned his head on my side. "In my travels, I've been looking for another way. I've talked to the most powerful witches and wizards all over the land. What I've been told is a rare book exists, one from the beginning of magic, and it has what I need to break the curse. The only magic I have left is to teleport, everything else is gone. What I need you for is to go with me, find the spell, and perform it. I've tried dozens of our kind and no one has gotten past the talking cat part, let alone agree to help me."

"So basically, I'm your default choice because no one else would?"

"No, Bellatrix. I've been watching you for a week now. I see how much you care for people, even when they turn their noses up at you. Yes, I know your magic is wonky at times, but I also see how powerful it is. You just need a different approach to learning to control it."

My jaw drops, and I sputter, "No, that can't be true. My entire family has written me off. They would have told me if I were powerful. I'm just a dud, Oliver."

He let out a hiss before speaking, "Your family knows nothing or knows something they are hiding. I was like you, things happening because it was too powerful for me to control. It took a very patient High Priestess to figure out it wasn't me screwing up, it was my magic being too strong. She taught me how to control it and before I was turned into this, my power rivaled hers."

"I don't know, Oliver. I think maybe you're seeing things in me that aren't there just because of your own experience." I pause before grumbling, "Not to mention the stalking me thing for a week is creepy."

Letting out a chuff, he replies, "I'm desperate and need to find someone to help me. You caught my attention merely by accident. I happened to be watching the Spring Solstice celebration when I heard a lot of shouting and swearing. Curiosity is part of my being, so I went to investigate. You were there with your red hair sticking up in the air, and candle wax all over you, along with the rest of the crowd. Some older man was yelling at you to just use matches next time, while several people surrounded you with wax droplets coating them too. I saw the tortured look on your face and it tugged at my heart. You have no idea how hard it was for me to not be able to interfere and take you out of there."

"That was the day I tried to light my candle, and it exploded on me. Well, on everyone around me. My father was so embarrassed, and really, I should have known better than to have tried it in public. Heck, I burned off my eyebrows last night trying to cook dinner. My father wasn't wrong." When the words left my lips, I didn't feel as sure of words that had been echoed to me for so many years.

"I can say with all honesty, it's not true and I can show you. Take a chance and come with me. I will teach you during our travels," he urges me, giving me puppy dog eyes. Well, actually kitty cat eyes.

I thought about my life and everything that had happened to me. My family and how they treat me, my prospects for the future, and how much I want to see the world outside of this little town. No matter how scared I am and don't want to admit he's right, Oliver's words feel right to me. "Okay."

"Okay?" he asks excitedly.

"When do we leave?" I say as I stand up and trip over the shoes I had removed during our talk. I spit out grass and dirt, my face flushing.

"This is going to be one interesting adventure with you, Bellatrix."

Arcadia

BY REBEL MORELLI & MK SAVAGE

T here was always that one defining moment in every Supernatural's life when they got their calling. For each Supernatural, that would happen on the day of their fourteenth birthday. Once we transitioned, the prestigious Arcadia Academy would invite us to attend. It's a moment we all looked forward to from the minute we learned what our fate would be.

My family was born of magic. My great-grandmother was one of the most powerful supernaturals of her time. The Donnachaidh name commanded respect. Every student received royal treatment from the teachers. My uncle Charlie had been one of the most powerful witches in centuries, bypassing all our families in sheer talent and raw power.

Just one year into the Academy, he impressed everyone enough to be offered a teaching apprenticeship upon finishing school. In his final year, the council approached him about joining. His future was sure to be incredible; he had finally had the courage to be open about his relationship with his roommate Eddie.

Unfortunately, a gay witch was something the world wasn't ready for. They had rescinded his position; shamed him, abused him, and the staff and council ignored him. But he was finally happy and didn't care about some bigoted old men.

On what would have been their one-year anniversary, Eddie and eleven other students vanished after a defense class. Twelve students vanished, and no one knew how or where they went. Everyone searched for months, but they couldn't find them.

As graduation day came closer, the search was called off. They didn't want any negativity affecting the academy, especially with the next generation of students arriving in a few weeks. It was as if Eddie and the other missing students had never existed. They banned all mention of them from the school grounds.

If anyone discussed or investigated the disappearance, the school authorities would expel them immediately. Charlie, however, had not given up. He had started his own investigation in secret, determined to find his partner; he wouldn't tell a soul though, too scared they would cast him out and he'd never be able to find his love.

Finally, the night before he was due to graduate, the bodies of Eddie and the missing students were, at last, found close to the Academy grounds. No longer could they ignore the horrible tragedy. The council would have to find out what had happened under their watch.

However, that was not the case. They announced the students had committed suicide. Each one was ashamed of something that would disgrace their families. They had ended their lives. It was an easy explanation for the council to give and it appeased everyone except Charlie.

Enraged at the lies and the disrespect they held for Eddie, Charlie had gone to Mr. Freidrickson, the Headmaster's, home to confront him. A few minutes after he arrived, Charlie shot him twelve times before turning the gun on himself. The community was in an uproar. The devastating incident scared the council, as they thought their beloved school was in danger.

They soon realized they had the perfect scapegoat and the following morning they announced that Charlie Donnachaidh had killed the missing students in a fit of jealous rage after finding out Eddie had left him for another. The brave Headmaster allegedly led him to his house intending to make him confess, but then Charlie brutally murdered him. Before Charlie had taken the coward's way out by ending his own life.

Not yet satisfied with blaming what could be an innocent man, they stated that no one with Donnachaidh blood would be permitted to practice magic ever again. They also claimed Charlie's victims would not receive proper justice, as he would never be brought to trial. Their next course of action would be the only way to honor them. With that decision made, our magic was then bound, and they banished us from the Academy.

It hurt our family; they were angry, and still wanted answers for what had caused Charlie, a brilliantly talented and extremely powerful witch, to snap and do what he did. The council who refused to even acknowledge their request ignored them. Until they received an anonymous package a few weeks after Charlie had died.

It was full of journals, letters, and files on the twelve missing students, the headmaster, and some very high-up members of the council. Hidden right at the back was a letter from Charlie explaining that he knew who had killed Eddie and the others. He stated no one would take action against so many powerful people, so he had to do something.

Unfortunately, he didn't say anything else but whatever happened that night left two people dead, a family in ruins, and had left the families of the murdered students with no real answers. For years, we were told stories about our uncle, of who he was and what had been done to him. No one in the family believed he had killed anyone, so they chose to remember the boy they loved, not the monster he was made to be. Even so, they taught us about our heritage and made us study magic. My grandmother would say that they could take our powers, but they could never take our knowledge.

I became obsessed with learning all I could about magic, my uncle, and what had happened at the Academy. However, all my gran would tell me when I would ask about it was that she took comfort in the fact he had died trying to do what was right and that one day all would be well again.

The world would know the truth. I would restore the Donnachaidh name to its former glory, and we would finally have justice for Charlie and the students whose deaths they covered up to protect those in power. Then and only then would he be finally at peace.

She had no idea how soon that would come though, because on my fourteenth birthday, on what should have been just an ordinary day, something amazing happened. For the first time in forty-eight years, a Donnachaidh received their powers.

The binding on my magic had been broken, sealing my fate. While the rest of my family's powers were still bound, mine ran free. The Council would now be forced to allow me to attend the Academy, as it stated in their laws that no Supernatural shall be allowed to live in the world unless they have completed all necessary training and schooling.

Finally, a Donnachaidh would be on school grounds, and I could finish what Uncle Charlie had started. I would get revenge for those who had been killed, I would clear my family's name, expose the lies and secrets surrounding the council and the academy. I wouldn't stop until every one of our blood had their powers back or I would die trying.

CHAPTER
One

ARIA - FOUR YEARS LATER

Pulling up at the academy, my mom's terror consumed me. She was shaking and frantically looked around her. It was almost as though she thought this was a trap and at any minute, the council would swoop down and take us away. Which, if I was being honest, that thought had gone through my mind a few times now.

It took a lot of work for us to get here. My great-grandmother, grandmother, and mom had fought, begged, and bargained. They worked to convince the council that since their binding had failed; I needed guidance to control the power growing inside me. There had been multiple meetings and who the heck knew what else just for them to even consider it.

Finally, after four long years, I received a call telling me they had accepted me and would enroll immediately. However, they explained that in no uncertain terms was any other member of my family allowed on the school grounds. Which was why we were currently sitting in my mom's car on the other side of the road, hidden away. I think if she hadn't felt so guilty about it, she would have made me take the bus.

Today was my eighteenth birthday and exactly fifty years since the students had vanished, I had planned it perfectly. It convinced the council I was unstable, that my powers were out of control, leaving me as an enormous risk to myself and others. After a long battle, the risk of exposing my magic or hurting a human was too great, and they reluctantly allowed me to enroll.

However, rather than the full acceptance of six years, I was to be given a year-to-year review. I didn't care about that, though. I wouldn't even need a year to expose them all. Plastering a smile on my face, I turned to my mom. Calming her down and making sure she got out of here safely came before anything else.

"Chill, mom. Everything's going to be okay. Nothing's going to happen to me. We both know the only reason I'm here is to clear the family name. Thanks to my great-grandma, I have more control of my powers than anyone else my age, and most adults as well. I'll be fine, I promise."

Every word I spoke was true. My great grandma has been teaching me magic ever since I was old enough to walk. Other kids played sports or did trivial things. I, on the other hand, studied and prepared, especially since my magic manifested.

"Don't make promises you can't keep, Aria. You're being thrown to the wolves. You won't just have to worry about the teachers. This isn't you starting out at entry level. These students have been there for years. They're the most advanced. Their powers will be right up there with yours. I just need to know you've thought this through."

Her voice quivered as she spoke, once again showing how worried she was about me being here. I had a feeling though that nothing I said would really help. The families here had ostracized us, and now I was going to be a part of them. She couldn't be here to help me because she wasn't allowed.

"It will be okay. I promise to call often, and you can text

me anytime now. Remember? I showed you how." I replied, even though I knew there was no way she would text me.

My mother was a lot of things, but being tech-savvy was definitely not one of them.

"I'll be worrying the entire time you're here. We're unsure about the treatment you'll receive here. This isn't just a small thing. This is fifty years of hatred and bigotry that you're going to have to deal with. Just try to keep your head down and find out everything that you can." She choked out before pulling my hand into hers. "I love you, Aria. Now get out of here before I change my mind and drive off with you still in the car."

"Love you too, mom. I'll call once I get settled in."

We both knew I wouldn't be calling. Not until I'd found the answers we were looking for, but those few paltry words would bring some comfort.

Getting out of the car, I glanced back once more to memorize her face. This may very well be the last time I saw her. Slamming the car door behind me, I got my suitcases and backpack from the trunk and headed toward the gates. I forced myself not to turn around until I heard the noise from the engine fade into nothing. I could do this. I had to do this. My family, my uncle, and those students needed justice and I would die trying to get it for them.

Steeling my nerves, I held my head high as I made my way through the wrought-iron gates. Looking around, I found the school grounds packed with students. I couldn't have picked a better time to turn up. My body burned with the feel of the heated stares as I walked by. The whispers about the Donnachaidh girl swirled in the air, making my stomach clench. And even though I'd hoped for at least a bit of time where no one knew who I was, I'd figured everyone here would, and this just confirmed it.

The giant double wooden doors were open when I passed through the entrance. Everyone stepped away from me, or sneered when I got too close. The whispers of the students seemed to get louder the further into the school I got. This place looked more like an old castle than a school. Which was probably because at one point they used it as a hideaway for some powerful Princess. Legend has it she fell in love with the wrong man, and they would meet here in secret. When they died, they turned it into the Academy.

Looking around, I finally found the sign stating new student admissions to the left and followed until it led me to a wooden door. I joined the small line and waited for my turn to go into the office.

"So, the rumors are true. They actually let a member of that scum-sucking murderous family back in the Academy. You have no place here and need to leave before Headmaster Hannigan sees you."

The whiny voice behind me had me cringing. It was the stuff of nightmares, and I really didn't want to see the face attached to it.

Turning around, I couldn't stop the laugh that burst out of me. She was, for lack of a better word, orange. I'm talking orange like the fruit or some Doritos from top to bottom. It was clear she had dipped into way too much self-tanner.

"What are you laughing at, freak?" She spat as I tried to reign in my giggles.

Her blonde hair and blue eyes just made the orange in her skin pop out even more.

"You? Had your threats been scarier and less comical, and if you didn't look like you had been swimming in a bag of Doritos. I wouldn't be laughing."

I laughed before turning back around and headed into what I assumed was the office since the line had moved.

"Name?" the woman at the desk said without looking up.

"Aria Donnachaidh," I stated, causing the woman to whip her head up and look at me. I was honestly surprised that she didn't get whiplash from that one single move.

"I was told to inform you that you would stay in your own room this year. We'll also be keeping a very close eye on you and if you get in trouble, you *will* be out of here. Now that's out of the way..." She punctuates with a firm nod. "... here's your schedule, and dorm assignment, along with your key. I would say it is good to have you, but that would be a lie. So please get out of my office," she said before looking back down at her computer, effectively dismissing me while making it quite clear I was not liked or even wanted.

What a bitch! I thought as I grabbed the papers and key off the desk and headed out of the room to find my dorm.

Luckily, I made it up with only scathing looks and mean whispers which I couldn't care less about. If they were going to scare me off, they would have to get a lot more creative.

CHAPTER
Two

ALARIC

My life had been planned out from the age of eight. I was determined to end the curse on my family after learning about my grandfather's death and would stop at nothing until I found a solution.

I had watched five of my brothers perish over the past five years. That left only three of us. I couldn't understand why our family risked having children only for them to be born male and have to watch them all die. When I asked my mom this, she just told me that when I fell in love, I would understand. Why, knowing her husband would die, did she risk it all to have a small piece of him still with her? Only two children born in the last fifty years had been female and all males had died before their thirtieth birthday, no matter what my grandfather had done, surely we had paid our dues now.

Years of planning, studying and sheer determination had resulted in me being the youngest Headmaster in history at twenty-two. Somehow, I had held the position for two years now. However, a little under a year ago, The Supernatural Council had called me in for a meeting.

With no ounce of compassion, they destroyed everything I

had believed was true. Informing me, the only way to break the curse was to get a Donnachaidh woman to fall in love with me. True love, which cannot be simulated with magic. This was why when Aria Donnachaidh's application for the school had come through, I fought to get her here. It was too much of a coincidence; she had to be the one who would save us.

A knock on the door snapped me out of my thoughts. I already knew who it was. No one else would dare disturb me while I was in this room.

"Come in, Kellan, and get it over with. I can hear your brain swirling from here."

There had been a time, not so long ago, that our families had been at war. An unspoken rule was that we should never mix our kinds. From the first day we met, Kellen and I formed an attachment, and he has been constantly by my side ever since.

After shutting the door behind him, he asked, "Why did you do it?"

I didn't have to explain myself to anyone, but I always confided in Kellan. However, this was the one time I couldn't. There was too much at stake.

"I had to Kellan. We couldn't very well let an untrained mage out into the world, could we? I am no happier about this than any of you, but I did what had to be done. Which means she gets to stay unless she chooses to leave. So, I suggest you and the guys just leave her be," I said, even though I knew it was a waste of breath.

Kellan was hard-headed and would do what he wanted, no matter what anyone told him. It had to be the angel in him.

"I'll just make sure she leaves then. Something must be wrong with her for the binding not to have worked, and I don't like it. We have all heard the horror stories of what

Charlie Donnachaidh did. We don't need another serial murderer on campus." He spat, clearly very passionate about everything that he said.

This was going to be harder than I thought.

"I really wish you would just let it be. It's going to be hard enough for me having her here. I don't need you and the guys getting in trouble."

I tried to reason with him one last time, even though I knew it wouldn't matter. He was stubborn through and through.

"We'll see. You can't protect her, though. It's already started and the girls in this school are going to bring her down. Apparently, Sarah caught her in the hall and told her she needed to leave, but all the Donnachaidh girl did was laugh and tell her she looked like a Cheeto or something. Now the others are out for blood."

Well, that was interesting, also very true. The *it* girls of the school were all vain and Sarah did indeed look very orange when I saw her earlier. It was hard to keep my laughter at bay.

"Well, there's nothing we can do now but see how it goes. The council's already breathing down my neck. I don't have time to worry about it."

I really hated lying to him, but if anyone found out I actually wanted her to be here, there would be hell to pay. So, I had to play the part, even though on the inside I was full of hope that my younger brothers could grow old.

"I'll leave you to it then, boss."

He chuckled, knowing I hated it when he called me that, as he strode out the door.

Heading over to the mirror on the back of my wall, I waved my hand over it and the Donnachaidh girl appeared. I had watched her ever since her mom petitioned to have her enrolled. Maybe it was curiosity or fear that something would stop her from coming. But every day I would check on her and with every detail I learned, a small part of me became hers.

She was my salvation; my life, and she would be mine. She just didn't know it yet.

CHAPTER

Three

ARIA

As soon as I shut the door to my dorm room, I dropped the bags and plopped myself down onto the bed. It has become clear to me this was going to be harder than I had thought. Sure, I'd watched enough television and listened when Gran had told me people would be awful to me. However, I'd expected it to slide off me and if I was being honest, it wasn't. It was irritating. People were so stuck in their ways they couldn't even believe I wasn't evil or looking to murder them.

"That woman is a heinous beast. I swear, if I was still in my human form, I would give her a piece of my mind. After all these years, a member of my family is finally here again, and she thinks she can talk to them that way. Uh-uh, not happening. I will so be peeing in her coffee tomorrow." A male voice sounded in my head, and I jerked upwards.

"What the fuck?" I shrieked, jumping from the bed. Looking around, I saw that there was a small red and white fox staring at me from the top of the desk.

"Oh no. Things are much worse than I ever could have envisioned. Me being gone has resulted in our gene pool becoming diluted with common muck. If you had muttered those words in my

day, young lady, why, I would have washed your dirty little mouth out with soap. Your mother shall be hearing from me. Well, once you finally clear my name, I can stop hiding as a disgusting animal."

The fox tilted his head and gave me what I could only describe as a mischievous look.

"Uh... what the hell is going on? No, stop talking, you're not real. This is some sort of game to get me to leave, right? Well nope, I'm here until I expose the cover-up that resulted in my uncle's death. Oh my god, why am I playing along with this crazy illusion?"

Shaking my head, I headed out the door. I wouldn't get any answers stuck in my room with whatever spell they had cast. I needed to explore before classes started.

To my chagrin, the damn fox followed me out. Was there no getting rid of this thing?

"I am truly sorry if I startled you. That was not my intention. It's hard, you see, when no one can know you exist. It's been miserable having to stay invisible for fifty years because if anyone finds you, they will rid your soul of the earth. I need your help so I can finally rest in peace and be with the ones I love. I swear to you, all of what I say is the truth, and if you look inside yourself, you will recognize me for who I am, just as I did with you."

Okay, so the creepy fox was right. I felt a bond towards him, but that could easily be the work of a powerful mage. It should be simple enough to work out, though.

"Okay, so you're saying you're my uncle? Then you should know this. What was it that Grandma used to make your toes fall off when you were kids?" I laughed, knowing there was no way this fox would know about this story.

"That is a trick, a brilliant one at that. It wasn't my toes; it was my fingers, and she used a spell from our mother's forbidden book of magic. My mom whooped her so badly she refused to speak for an entire week."

If foxes could smirk, that's what this one would be doing

right now. It completely floored me he was telling the truth. I came to avenge his death and this whole time; he was here.

"Explain now, or so help me, I'll skin your..." I wave my hands at him wildly. "... ghost-like ass... fox ghost ass?" I let out a sigh and rolled my eyes at the creature. "Well, whatever you are, I'll skin you. Have you any idea what your death did to your mom? To your sister? Grandma still talks about how she failed you. How you'd still be alive if she hadn't gotten pregnant and left the Academy? There better be a great explanation because we had to suffer all these years for something we had no idea about," I said, shock and astonishment laced my voice.

"I could go into detail about that night, but honestly, we don't have time right now. Just know this: your being here has put a price on your head. There are many people here who were a part of the killings all those years ago. We need to be careful about all of this because two students have already been reported missing and you will not be next. I must go. I have been watching the council members for the past few weeks and they are hiding something. You must do one thing, though. After classes start, go to the old library. It's at the top of the Academy. Once you get there, head to the fantasy section and look for a book by Charle. P. Emerson. Inside, you will find all you need to assist you in clearing my name. Can you do this for me, for our family?"

Before I could reply, he was gone. Stupid fox, he could have answered some of my questions before disappearing. I guess now, all I could do was wait until classes started two days from now or I could check it out. Decisions, decisions.

Why wait? I thought before heading out of the dorm building.

There were no rules about not exploring campus, so if anyone stopped me, I had an excuse. Once again, the sight of the school awed me. It was so old-school and elegant. I couldn't believe I was actually here.

Heading through the double doors once again, I noticed

most of the people who had been here earlier had dispersed, which actually worked out in my favor. Striding down the main hallway, I noticed the wooden circular stairs that hopefully led to the top floor of the academy. I didn't know why I didn't grab my map.

Oh, wait. Yes, I did. It had to do with the talking fucking fox.

Finally, after climbing about a billion stairs, I reached the top. God, who puts a library all the way up here? No wonder people read on kindles now. You needed to be a star athlete to get a dang book.

Annoyed at how unfit I was, I pushed open the door and stomped in. Instantly, I knew I was in the wrong place. The huge, gorgeous tank of a man glaring down at me was a pretty good sign.

"Mason, someone needs to come take out the trash before it infects the dorm. I would do it, but who knows where this thing has been," he said, looking at me as if I was the dirtiest thing he had ever seen.

Well, that just took him straight from gorgeous to asshole status in less than a minute.

Before I could give this douchebag a piece of my mind, a tall, dark, and handsome guy was suddenly standing there in the doorway. His eyes flashing red was the last thing I saw before he threw me from the room. My head smashed down on the concrete floor, pain flared through my body and darkness consumed me.

CHAPTER

Four

ARIA

"**Y**ou know he's going to kill you, right? He specifically said no getting into trouble and what do you do? You almost kill the one person they ordered us to stay away from. What the fuck is wrong with you? Our reputation here is already awful enough as it is. We cannot be associated with shit like the Donnachaidh," an unfamiliar deep voice said as I came to.

My head was still pounding, and my throat felt as if it was the Sahara Desert.

"Water?" I croaked, opening my eyes to find myself surrounded by five of the most attractive guys I had ever seen. Looking at each of them, my eyes flashed when I noticed one was the asshole who had been at the door when I entered.

"We ain't getting her no water. She needs to leave." Another voice said, and it was the guy who had thrown me through the door.

Fuck this shit! I thought as I flung out my hands.

All the surrounding men shot back and slammed into walls behind them, hanging there as if by invisible strings as I slowly stood up watching them with wary eyes. The eyes I knew were glowing but didn't care about. Leaving them there, I strutted into their kitchen to get a drink. Their shouts and angry words followed me.

That'd show them.

I figured I would have to deal with people being assholes, but I hadn't been prepared for physical attacks. From now on, I'll ensure that doesn't happen again. Walking back into the hall, I took a moment to study the men who had decided I was trash just because of my name.

The one closest to me was shorter than the rest. He still towered over me, though, since I was a mere five-foot-two. He had short fiery red hair and emerald eyes that at this moment were staring at me as if I was crazy.

A snapping noise brought me out of my examinations. My eyes flicked over to the guy who had thrown me from the room. His long blond hair billowed behind him as he fell from the wall to land on his feet.

"Is that the best you got?"

He laughed before flicking a wrist again and letting the other guys loose. The smirk on his face growing with his inflated ego.

"Oh please, if I wanted you hurt, you wouldn't be talking right now. Unlike you mindless sheep, I haven't lived by the council's pathetic rules my whole life. I have ways to hurt you that your tiny little brains could never comprehend. A word of advice, though, you should never believe everything you hear. People can always surprise you," I said before shooting them all one last look. "Gotta bounce."

I felt the tell-tell shiver go through my body as I teleported myself back to my room. As soon as I left the hall, my emotions got the better of me. Snapping my fingers, I took all their clothes, even the ones from their rooms. It was a harmless prank, but it was definitely going to cause issues.

Fuck, I thought as I tried not to scream.

My head was pounding from where it had hit the wall. It

was bad enough that everyone hated me, but now I had acted without thinking. They could get me kicked out, and that couldn't happen. Not until I had proved my family's innocence. One of these days, I was going to have to control my temper.

Turning around, I saw that all their clothing was burning in the fireplace. Well, I wasn't going to be giving those back. At least there would be no proof I was the one who had done it. I would have to make sure this was a reminder to them to not screw with me. This place was not safe for me, though, and these people didn't care if I lived or died. Wait... that's not right. They wanted me, and everyone else in my family, dead. No, I would not make the mistake of trusting anyone or giving them any ammunition to use against me. No matter how hot they were or how nice of an ass they had.

The only upside about them segregating me from everyone else and giving me one of the oldest dorms here was I could be myself and think. In here, I could be vulnerable and not worry about anyone hurting me or discovering my plans.

Looking at the suitcase on the floor, I sighed. I could put everything up with magic, but I had nothing better to do. So, I hung up my clothes and got my room in order. All the old journals and folders of the missing kids sat on my desk, staring at me. I had already read them so many times; I pretty much had everything memorized.

"I told you not to go to the library until classes started!" My uncle's condescending voice filled me, causing me to jump.

"I didn't want to wait. I really don't want to be here any longer than I have to be. Pretty sure I learned my lesson on that though and hopefully, those assholes learned not to touch women too," I said, kinda wishing I had listened to him.

"Those assholes, as you so eloquently put it, guard the library. The path to it runs through their house. Which is something I would

have told you before classes started, but no, my only family member to grace the school since me is apparently an idiot? Sneak in during classes. I am assuming you can do a simple unlock spell."

His words hurt a bit more than they should because I had let my impulsiveness take over and they could have seriously hurt me.

"I'm sorry. I won't do it again and, of course, I can do a simple unlock spell," I said, meaning every word.

Before he could answer, there was a loud banging on my door. Walking over, I looked in the peephole and saw a sculpted, naked chest that made me want to drool. Pulling the door open, I smirked at the asshole who had thrown me through the door.

It was one thing to learn a lesson, but a whole other thing for him to know I did. So, the smirk stayed in place.

"What do you want?" I asked, knowing full well what he was going to say, especially since I was having a hard time keeping my eyes from traveling his well-built, partly unclothed body. It was a lot harder than I would ever admit to.

"Where are our clothes? I know it was you," he spat at me.

He was clearly angry, but I struggled to hold back my laughter. It was hard to take him seriously when he was stark-ass naked. And equally hard to keep my hands to myself when what I really wanted to do was run my fingers over his wash-board abs.

"They're gone. Maybe next time you'll think before throwing a random person through a doorway. Oh, and my name is Aria, not the Donnachaidh girl," I said as I moved to close the door, only to have him stick his foot in it to keep it from shutting.

"You'll regret this, trash, You've no idea who you're messing with," he gritted out before turning and striding down the hall, thereby giving me a full view of his muscular ass. What a fine ass it was.

CHAPTER
Five

ARIA

My stomach growling forced me out of the room the next day. Since the asshole had come to my door, I'd been pouring over the files of the missing students. I'd already done this so many times, but I wanted to be as prepared as I could be.

To me, it looked like a cover-up, but from what or even why, I had no idea. My uncle had never shown back up, so I'd been unable to ask him. What the hell could be so important that he stayed away when he could finally talk to someone?

Nevertheless, I was now headed to the cafeteria. Walking down the hallways, people stepped out of my way, but no one approached me. I kept an eye out for the guys, but luckily, I hadn't seen them. Hopefully, I could get in, get my food, and get the hell out.

The second I walked into the cafeteria; everything went quiet. So much for getting in and getting out. Every eye was on me as I lined up to get a tray. They laid copious amounts of food out buffet style, but I just grabbed a cheeseburger and fries. I wanted to get out of there as quickly as possible because some of those stares were burning figurative holes in my body.

Slowly, as I made it through the cavernous space, various conversations resumed, however I heard my name sneered more than a few times. It was hard to keep my mouth shut, but I somehow managed it.

"That's all?" The woman behind the register said as she looked me up and down.

If the look on her face said anything, then she was also someone who didn't want me there.

"Yes," I replied, barely keeping the anger out of my voice.

It was seriously pissing me off. I couldn't even get lunch without an attitude. Turning to head back to my room, I stopped quickly, almost tripping over my feet. In front of me stood two of the assholes from the room.

Fuck, I need to get out of here.

Stealing my spine, I acted as if they were of no consequence and resumed my lonely journey. Too bad one of them stepped into my path.

"Well, looky here. Who let this trash in?" One of them asked as I started counting in my head and attempted to step around him for him to just move over back in front of me.

Don't say anything, don't play their game.

I just knew this was going to be the new mantra I'd have to play in my head. I attempted to keep the anger out of my face.

"I don't want any problems," I tried to say as peacefully as possible, but it probably came out as more of a warning. Didn't matter. The look in their eyes told me they were going to start trouble, regardless.

"If you didn't want any problems, you should have stayed home with the rest of your pathetic family! Get used to this because we've been nice so far, but things will get worse if you don't leave," he shouted, in my face as I attempted to keep myself from slamming the tray in my hands over his head.

"I'm not going anywhere," I uttered between clenched

teeth, wanting nothing more than to get out of the cafeteria without any more fuss, but everyone fell silent once again.

With that said, I knew I'd laid out the gauntlet, and they were going to try to push me out, but I wouldn't allow it. I could take anything they threw at me.

"Oh, trust me you will," he growled at me before throwing his hand down on my tray, knocking it out of my hand. He swaggered away, the other guy following him.

What the fuck? Were they raised without manners?

I was unable to hold in my gasp at the rage in his eyes. His hatred for me burned through him and showed up as a fire lighting his eyes. Somehow keeping myself from turning and watching them walk away, I waved my hand. Freezing the falling burger and fries midair, I willed them and the tray back into my hand. Sometimes I was so thankful for my magic because I needed to get the hell out of there before my temper took over. What kind of fucked up people tried to waste food?

"Thanks for the practice," I replied, the stark clear in my tone as I walked out of there without looking back. It was harder than hell to do because I didn't want them behind me, but if I showed that, then they would win.

As soon as I was out of the cafeteria, I hauled ass back to my room. My mind raced at the thought of how I was going to sneak around with everyone being out to get me. When I closed the door to my dorm room, I was panting.

"What happened?" My uncle's voice said in my head, causing me to look around until I spotted his fox form sitting on my desk beside my notes.

"Just people being dicks, nothing I can't handle," I stated, somehow keeping the concern that I felt to myself.

Things here were just going to get harder, but that just meant I was going to have to be better, try harder.

"You are a Donnachaidh. We will restore our name and then we will make them all pay. I found out something pretty interesting

today. For some reason, the headmaster is very interested in the Donnachaidh, or in particular, you. Be careful because I won't have anything bad happening to you under my watch."

The last bit sounded sad, and my heart ached for him. How terrible must it have been for him to lose his love in such a tragic way?

I didn't reply as I walked over and ran my hand over his fur. No matter how I looked at it, they stacked the odds against us, but that didn't mean anything. There was no going back until I had cleared our name.

The need burned through me at the thought, and I didn't tamp it down. If I had any hopes of succeeding, I would need all the fury burning through me. Everyone would pay. Especially the ones responsible.

Six

ARIA

Yesterday had flown by and luckily, I hadn't had any more run-ins with anyone. I stayed in my dorm as much as possible to avoid the guards, or as I dubbed them in my head, the assholes. I had given in and called home. Hearing my mom's voice had calmed my nerves some since my run-in with the guys. She still had some worries, but I think she was mostly convinced that everything was going okay. I may have left out the run-in with the human Dorito and assholes as well as meeting my uncle. That could wait until everything was over. She would pull me out so fast if she knew the truth. But I couldn't let that happen. I was more determined than ever to finish this.

"Classes start today. Did you memorize your schedule? If you listen to me, I can get you to the library. You should have a free period when the other guards shall be in class. That will be your opportunity. Oh, one thing before you go. Be careful after all is said and done... yes, I would like to be free, but I will not have another innocent life taken to ensure my freedom. Do not take any unnecessary risks and for all that is holy in this world, avoid the guards and our dutiful headmaster at all costs," He whispered the last part,

and I could see just how much the death of the students had affected him.

Losing a loved one was always hard, but their story was just tragic.

"Okay, I promise to be careful, but I'm not giving up. It's not just our family who deserve the truth," I replied, before turning away from him.

Grabbing my bookbag laying against my desk, I headed out. I wasn't going to waste any more time and risk being caught again. Now that I knew where I was going, I could just teleport there and save my poor legs from climbing all those damn stairs. But not until I was sure the assholes wouldn't be there.

Lost in thought, I made my way to magic history class. I had a feeling it wasn't going to be a fun one, considering the events that trashed the Donnachaidh name would be a popular subject.

The whispers of the other students got louder the closer I got to the class. This was going to get irritating fast. Everyone gave me a wide berth though keeping at least two feet of space between me and them as if I was diseased. That part didn't bother me. I wasn't here to make friends.

Just as I found the classroom I needed to be in, I fell. My foot had hit something, and I went down like a sack of potatoes. Luckily, I got my hands out in time to keep my face from bashing the floor. However, howls of laughter overtook the hallway as I looked around to see what I had tripped over. A large foot, attached to an even larger man who was a giant asshole, took up my vision.

Mason, I think, was what he had been called.

Don't kill him, Aria. Don't do it! I thought as I pulled myself up from the floor.

"Oops, didn't see you there," he said smirking, causing another round of laughter to go through the sizable crowd that had gathered.

Without uttering a single word, I took a page out of his book and walked right up to him. With a smile plastered across my face, I kicked the shit out of his shin before turning and heading into my classroom. His cursing chased me as I entered the classroom, and my giggle slipped out before finding a seat in the back corner of the classroom.

"Well, well, well, I didn't think we would see you again so soon and here, of all places. Do you understand your family history is a huge part of the curriculum here? I feel you have an unfair advantage."

Ugh! The voice was pure sex. Deep, smooth, and my insides melted at the sound. Looking up to see who the voice belonged to, all attraction fled when I saw one of the asshole guards.

"What, didn't get enough last time? It's good to see you've found some clothes, though. A body like yours needs to be hidden away so as not to terrify small children."

Plastering on my best *'you disgust me face'*, I turned away from him and pulled out my textbooks. Hoping he would get the hint and just leave, but no, it seemed I wouldn't be that lucky. He pulled out the seat next to me and wordlessly sat beside me.

I tried really hard to just ignore him, but the heat from his eyes burned into me throughout the whole lesson. On my life, I could not tell you a word the teacher said, and it was getting on my nerves. Turning to face him, I was just about to give him a piece of my mind, but he beat me to it.

"You being here hurts my best friend, and that's something I won't tolerate. You may think you're a little badass. But babe, I guarantee by the time I'm done with you, you're going to wish you were as dead as your uncle."

His words hurt, but nothing could prepare me for the pain that came next. I had about two seconds to wonder what he was talking about before my body started to shake. The pain shot up my legs like fire, causing me to cringe and grit my teeth.

"What have you done?" I ground out before the pain exploded in my head like a blinding light.

It was as if someone had taken needles dipped in a burning poison and poked them through my skin.

Screaming out, I fell out of the chair, but the pain from whatever spell he used was so bad, I didn't feel the hit to the ground. Just when the torture was at its worst and I saw spots, it dissipated. Leaving just as quickly as it had started.

"That was just a small taste of what will happen if you stay here. Either leave of your own free will, or leave in a box like the last Donnachaidh before you," he whispered before brushing off his pants and heading out of the classroom.

"Miss Donnachaidh, you need to go to the office! Now!" the teacher yelled as I was trying to pull myself up.

Not one person helped me. I knew things wouldn't be easy, but to sit by while someone was being tortured was beyond my comprehension. Pulling myself up finally, I didn't even look at the teacher before squaring my shoulders and marching my sore body out of the room.

I hadn't even bothered to pick up my things. I just left before the tears fell, refusing to show any weakness. The headmaster's office I already knew was at the top of the east tower. Far from the classrooms and dorms, it was settled at the back of the school. I dragged my feet, my body screamed with each step. Hopefully, we could get my punishment over quickly and I could go home and rest.

A horrible sense of dread filled me with each step as I neared the office. This man would hate me more than any other person in the school. He believed my uncle had killed his grandfather and those students. This wasn't going to go well, but could anything really be worse than the pain I had just gone through?

One thing was certain, though. Before I left here, I would find that asshole and make him pay for what he had done.

Before I knew it, I was standing in front of a huge, black steel door. Headmaster Hannigan was plastered across it.

The door swung open, and my eyes snapped up. In front of me was a man who could only be described as a god. I didn't have a chance to say a word before he grabbed my arm and pulled me inside. The only sound was the slamming of the door behind him.

Epilogue

Council Member Alderton

Well, that couldn't have gone better if I tried. Who knew that worthless mage would come in handy? The Donnachaidh girl was being pushed at Alaric even faster than we thought. Years of planning, years of death and destruction, had finally led to this moment. Seeing the worry on the other council member's face melt away gave me a sense of gratification that I hadn't felt in years. With Alaric's looming death, he would be more determined than ever to make the Donnachaidh girl fall for him, and when she did, our plan would finally be complete.

The prophecy had told of a baby born of magic. A baby of Hannigan and Donnachaidh blood that will hold the ultimate power. Finally, after all these years of pilfering pathetic powers from unworthy vessels, we could be free. Yes, draining the power from the chosen child would result in eternal youth. We would cement our places at the top of the supernatural council and once and for all, we would rule all.

Jenée Robinson

Jenée Robinson has been married for over 20 years now, has three ornery girls, and lives on a cattle farm.
Writing has always been one of her loves and she's excited to see where it takes her.
She has completed several books, short stories, and has more releasing soon. She is busy writing more, as well as more novellas and books.
Other than writing, she loves reading and photography.
She's a Harry Potter Nerd and loves the show Supernatural and Captain America.

You can follow her here:

FB Reader Group:
www.facebook.com/groups/faefulreaders

Bookbub:
www.bookbub.com/authors/jenee-robinson

facebook.com/jeneerobinsonauthor
twitter.com/jeneer82
instagram.com/jeneerobinson82

Other books by Jenée:

The Creeper Saga
Fate of the Fate

Jupiter Dresden

Jupiter is just a small town girl with big dreams. She loves to travel with her husband. She's a mother & cat lover. Anything paranormal has always fascinated her, as well as writing, so it's only natural she'd mix the two.

You can follow her here:

Facebook:
Jupiters Journey
Amazon:
Jupiter Dresden
Instagram:
authorjupiterdresden
TikTok:
@authorjupiterdresden

Other books by Jupiter:

The Curse Of Winchester
<u>Operation Ann</u>
<u>Gifted Curse (Co-write with Rinna Ford)</u>
<u>Goddess Of Flames</u>
<u>Hunter (Co-write with Jenée Robinson)</u>
Abandon Hope (Co-write with Jenée Robinson & Evelyn Belle)
Sam's Secret
Hidden Truths Of Ravenwood

Defending Skullpass (Co-write with Evelyn Belle)
Sinners Playground (April 2024)

Anthologies:
Melissa & The Lost Tomb of Akila
Always Dreaming
With This Axe
Mania's Death (Co-write with Miki Ward)
A Date With Death (Co-write with M. Lizbeth)
Drina
My Zombie Girlfriend
Heart Of A Hunter

M. Calder

Melody Calder is a multi-trope romance author with an addiction to chocolate, books, and swearing, not necessarily in that order. Her mind is always full of interesting characters and plot twists. She not-so-secretly loves cliffhangers and likes to write ones that aren't the norm. Also has an annoying habit of using the word "that." She hopes to survive the teenage years of her twins and life with her handsy husband and dog, who lives up to his name of Dragon.

Stuck in the Midwest for now, she hopes to move somewhere where the cold doesn't hurt her face. She has an extensive collection of elephant figurines and loves to craft in her almost nonexistent spare time. Her family and friends will tell you she needs reminders for everything, especially putting the clothes in the dryer, but they love her anyway. She should come with a warning label that says, "Will say inappropriate things often."

Standalones
Dance For Me
Coming Undone
Scandal
Heartbreaker
Losing Faith

Standalones in Shared Worlds
Yin

Depths of Glory

MK Savage

MK Savage is an urban fantasy/paranormal husband–wife writing duo who enjoy creating the books they would want to read. They live in Southern California where they're ruled by their two cats who expect to be worshiped as gods.

When they're not researching the viability of the steamy scenes they write, you can find them at the beach or their favorite coffee shop creating their next romance.

Want more MK Savage?
https://linktr.ee/mksavage

Also by MK Savage:

THE DEVIL'S WHOREHOUSE SERIES

Jade
https://books2read.com/u/3nDkAB

Harlow Banks Rejected Mates Series

Soul Bound
https://geni.us/HarlowBanks1

Rebel is a single mother of three demons, from a small town where nothing ever really happens outside of a writer's mind. A huge lover of books, she started to follow her favorite indie authors on social media. Fast forward a few years and she finally felt like she had found her people. Writing was never something she thought she could do. School was hard, and her teachers were critical but some amazing author friends convinced her it was time to share the crazy dark stories from her mind with the world.

A huge lover of the Supernatural, and all things dark and twisted, she has big plans for future stories and will never stick to just one genre or trope. Her mind is truly something scary and the stories she has planned will definitely leave you on the edge of your seats. From cowrites, anthologies, shared worlds and more the next few years are going to be interesting.

A self-proclaimed snobby reader she vows to give her readers different, engaging stories that push the boundaries of the normal author. Never one to back down from a challenge Rebel is one of her and her co-authors biggest critics always determined to be better and do more.

When she isn't busy with her children, working, or writing she will usually be stalking cover groups for pretties or trolling Instagram for inspiration. If you want to keep up with Rebel, come stalk her by clicking on the link below. She loves nothing more than discussing books and ideas with like-minded readers.

https://linktr.ee/rebelmorelli

Made in the USA
Columbia, SC
20 October 2023

24720388R00069